Long is the Way and Hard

Also by Rose Helen Mitchell and published by Ginninderra Press
Siege of Contraries
Pilgrim Souls
Whispering Shadows
Across Time (Pocket Poets)
James Joyce (Pocket Polemics)
My Linwood (Pocket Places)
Pasha (Pocket People)

Rose Helen Mitchell

Long is the Way and Hard

To the memory of Joseph James McAninch
1965–1967

Long is the Way and Hard
ISBN 978 1 76041 811 3
Copyright © Rose Helen Mitchell 2019
The source and author of the blessing on pages 42–43 are unknown –
anecdotal history

First published 2019 by
GINNINDERRA PRESS
PO Box 3461 Port Adelaide 5015
www.ginninderrapress.com.au

Long is the way and hard,
that out of Hell leads up to light.

Milton, *Paradise Lost*, Book II 432–433

Glossary

ahint	behind, at the back of
ain	own, as in 'it is my own…'
alang	along
ane	one
bealin'	furious, foaming at the mouth
breenged	forced way through a door, crowd
bumphly	comfortable, soft
dumbfounert	dumbfounded
fae/frae	from
fach	bother, as in 'don't worry about that'
freens	friends
glaikit	silly, foolish, not able to think clearly, distracted
gloaming	twilight
guid	good
hauns	hands
hiv	have
ken	know
louping	leaping, clumsy dancing
mair	more
mebbe	maybe
nae	no or none
nyaff	upstart
ramganshen	clumsy, like a bull in a china shop
skiting	moving fast, as in a dish slipping on a polished surface
snell	bitter cold, as in snow wind
spalpeen	rascal
speer	to enquire, understand
trachles	concerns, troubles
wan	one
wance	once

Prologue

When news of the November 1918 Armistice reached Australian cities and towns, cathedral bells rang all day declaring sounds of hope and peace. Officials hoisted the Union Jack high on public buildings. Harbours reverberated with the sounds of sirens and hooters from tugboats, steamships and all kinds of watercraft. The weariness of war flew from the streets and paddocks like a murder of crows taking flight. Workers went on holiday. At city street corners, the Salvation Army band played 'God Save the King' while the heartbroken dressed in black and mourned their losses. Prime Minister Billy Hughes declared a holiday for high school students. He extended the closure of lower grades until 13 November because of the influenza epidemic that raged and travelled along the railway lines to towns and country settlements.

In every city and town, throngs of the hopeful waited at train stations, bus terminals and docksides. They stood on platforms decorated with bunting listening for the sound of engines, the hiss of steam and for the first glimpse of a loved one. Banners blaring 'Welcome Home' waved above them and officials paced nervously in corners. People stopped in groups on the streets to sing their hearts out. After the Armistice, world leaders sought retribution and restitution while national boundaries were realigned.

Hospital ships, reassigned as transport, carried troops returning home to places far, far away from the horrors of Europe. Australian boys returned as men – some ravaged by blood, gore and gas. They gloried in the wide big skies and sunshine of their country. They shed the mud of France and the fog of grey English skies like snakes shedding skin. Country boys returned to the husbandry of farms and fence-building and sumptuous home cooking and town boys fitted themselves into jobs that would provide financial security. They found opportunities to learn useful skills and a place in a familiar community. A grateful lucky few had girlfriends waiting for them. Bonds of friendship and mateship stayed locked in the hearts of men who'd pulled through the shelling and gassing and relentless enfilade. Promises to keep in touch after the war were fervent and profuse.

Limbless and faceless young men in wheelchairs studied the greenery of trees in foreign hospital gardens and thought of the blackened sticks in the French forests they'd left behind. Young women stopped knitting balaclavas and socks and directed their efforts to the comfort and care of returned veterans. Some fulfilled their pre-war promises of marriage and motherhood.

In cottages and tenements and manor houses and farmhouses, mothers, fathers, wives, brothers and sisters looked with sad longing at framed photographs of uniformed young men who would never come home. Letters they'd received from the front lines were read again and again until the folds in the paper split from too much handling. When reports of the carnage of the trenches were publicised, they looked at each other in bewilderment, and asked why? How could this massacre take the title of the *Great* War?

While the planet turned on its axis, ignorant of the blundering brutality committed on its crust, options for individual futures were considered. Decisions made, and executed with bold courage, strengthened the resolve of migrants who sought new lives in countries like Canada, New Zealand and Australia, and the world settled into a fever of post-war reconstruction. In Ireland, the tribal fight for independence was relentless. Some families grew tired of the continual shootings and hatred and sought a more peaceful life in England and in Scotland.

Before

Christmas 1919
Langley, Berks

Dear Harry

I'm sorry to bring you the sad news that Patrick died on Christmas Eve. Before he died, he asked me to send you these few mementos of the times you shared with him in the war. He was anxious you should know that your friendship sustained him during your visit here. For Pat, the last few months were filled with pain, doctors and surgery. He limped his weariness through days and nights. He coughed. He sobbed. He resigned himself to dying. I will always miss him but I could never wish him back to the terrible suffering of this last year.

There has been one truly happy event. Patrick and I got married in June. It was a quiet affair. There's more – I am due to have his baby in March next year. What a wonderful memorial to Pat that will be. We are all busy knitting and sewing for this new little person whose name will honour my husband.

Although Patrick had difficulty speaking, he did manage to tell me through handwritten notes about happier times he'd shared with you in spite of the war. Like the time he learned the tricks of two-up and especially about the hilarity of the frog race that you organised. Do you remember last Christmas when you were here and Kate thumped tunes on the piano? We sang 'Pack Up Your Troubles' and 'It's a Long Way to Tipperary' and you recited Banjo Paterson's 'Santa Claus in the Bush' – all twenty-three verses. Do you remember? I do. It was the happiest time for all of us and especially for Pat. After you sailed for home, his health never really picked up, except for a brief period when we exchanged our wedding vows. After that, he became despondent and lost the will to write and eventually, in spite of his happiness about the baby, the will to live. Please know that we are indebted to you. I hope repatriation has been easy for you. It would be wonderful to hear from you about how things are in your life now. Perhaps one day in the future, our paths will cross again.

Love to you and to yours from a grateful friend.

Caitlin O'Hare

Harry

I took my time opening the package. I tried not to think too much about the last time I'd seen Patrick but images of him out of breath, struggling with speech, eating and drinking, were vivid. Inside the package was a full-face balaclava with a note:

I know you'll say, what do I want with a bloody balaclava in an Australian summer? – It's to remind you of the night of *The Great Race of the Frogs*, when we got drunk, ate apples and sung ourselves hoarse. The night we stumbled over the dying German. The night we buried him.

The tobacco tin was tucked inside. It also had a note stuck to it.

Hey. Harry! Remember we fought over this? Well, you can have it now. I traced Karl Grottenthaler's mother and mailed the letters, photos and rosary I took from Karl that night in the war. For some reason, I couldn't part with the tin. The decision is yours now. Her address is Frau Grottenthaler, Bergenstrasse 42, Garmisch, Germany 3926.

The edges of the tin were smooth. I imagined that Patrick had kept it in a pocket and friction between fabric and metal had rounded the corners. Karl's leave passes still nestled inside.

I touched them, closed the lid and held the tin close to my chest. It felt warm; the way a friendship sometimes does when the conditions that shaped the bond lie back in the past.

Nina

At 42 Bergenstrasse, Garmisch, Southern Germany, Frau Grotten-thaler sat on the edge of her dead son's bed. She held an open package in her hands. Sobs poured from the depth of her soul. She picked at the edges of the wrapping paper and a loud long 'Aaaagh! bounced off the walls of the little room. She grabbed a rosary that sat on top of other things. She crushed it to her breast and flung herself onto the bed, where she lay until black night replaced the grey day.

Before the war, she had loved working in her garden. Each season, she'd gathered fruits and vegetables that grew in her small patch. She pickled beetroot, and made jam from blackberries and blackcurrants. At the end of each preserving project, Nina stood in front of the open pantry door admiring the result of her work. One of her great pleasures in life was making a sponge cake for Karl's dessert, decorating it with blueberries in winter, then watching him devour it with youthful pleasure. Nina had ambitions that one day she'd have a little shop and people would come from miles away to buy her preserves and jams. In the instant she received the news that Karl had died, her dream died. It now lay in shattered shards like the broken bits of her heart.

Lettie

In the Australian town of Numurkah, Victoria, the wondrous telephone and electricity had been installed in most businesses and some houses, and motorcars were fast replacing horse transport. At 47 Meiklejohn Street, Lettie Kenihan thumped a mass of bread dough for the third and last time. The smell of yeast tickled at her nose and a loose curl of dark hair sat like a question mark on her left cheek. As she worked at the day's supply of bread, she sang an old Scottish song of farewell.

> 'Will ye no' come back again,
> Will ye no' come back again
> Better lo'ed ye cannae be,
> Will ye no' come back again?…'

The words trailed away. A tear slid from her eyes. She leant over the dough and sighed the longest deepest sigh. Lettie had given up all religious affiliations many years ago, but she had her own style of prayer. She raised her eyes to the ceiling and called out, 'Are ye up there, Hughie? Are ye listenin' tae me? Gie my boy something tae hope for. I want tae see him laughin' and whistlin' his way through the days, like he used tae. It would be a good thing tae see him full o' love for some decent clean woman. He needs that. Are ye listenin', Hughie? what we all need is hope and that's all I'm askin' for.' She covered the dough with a clean tea towel, rolled down her sleeves and toddled along the hall to her sewing corner.

Caitlin

In a two-storey house in Langley, Berkshire, Caitlin O'Hare stood by a white-painted wicker cradle. A lace frill trimmed the edge of the hood. A glistening white pillow and sheet filled the space where her baby would lie. The scent of spring sunshine floated around her from the newly ironed linen.

When I first came to live in this house as a refugee from the death of my parents, and through the nights when Patrick was away at war, I liked to lie in his bed and listen to the creaks and groans of the house timbers and the window-tapping branches of the chestnut tree in the yard. Now, when I lie there, I try to capture the sound of Pat's voice and the smell of him. I link each image of Patrick to something once familiar; a walk, a game, a dance, a voice. It's as if I borrow an event or thing to give the times credibility or power.

Sometimes I think his voice is answering my questions: How are you? I ask, and imagined responses overflow my thoughts. Sometimes I stand with hands beseeching towards the past and I remain uncomforted. In all my early memories of Patrick, he is laughing and singing, or reciting lines from Donne, Milton or some modern author like Forster. I want to speak with him. I want to touch his beautiful face. I want to feel his strong long fingers stroke my hair. I want to hear his voice. What would it say? Once, I heard him quote a line from Donne – a sonnet, I think: 'Batter my heart, three person'd God…' That is how my heart feels. It's been punched and battered to a pulp. Patrick had been a living poem.

Sometimes, when I want to block out the dark days, I make myself remember the good times of the past. One fond memory I turn to is the image of Pat climbing a wall to steal apples from old Mr Wilson's orchard. They were the sweetest apples. Ever.

The baby inside Caitlin seemed to know that she was thinking of its father and gave two strong kicks as if to say, 'I'm here. I will comfort you.'

1

Caitlin

My darling Patrick

Our baby has just kicked the writing pad off my belly. Would you believe that now?

I write this with the hope that it will bring you closer to me. To feel your arms around me and hear your voice again would be blissful. Tonight, I am alone and thinking about the time you returned from France. That first sight of you made holes in my heart that nothing has ever filled. I still see your beautiful face smashed to a gnarled network of bunched-up skin and bone and your body bent almost double like that of a broken old man. I'd seen the sinister cost of patriotism around the streets, and at my work with the Red Cross. Young men with crutches, disfigured, limbless. What on earth was it all for? Why are there so many of them?

Your mother and your sisters have been a great source of comfort to me. They allow me space enough to weep. Molly and Bridie listen when I talk about my mixed feelings of gratitude for having known you and heartbreak for losing you. Patrick, if you were here beside me now, what would we be saying to each other? Perhaps you'd sing for me. Perhaps you'd teach me some of the French phrases you learned in your time away. Perhaps you'd say, '*Je voudrais un heure baisement vous.*' And I'd plead ignorance and bring you a glass of water. Perhaps we'd stand by our baby's cradle and sing soft Irish lullabies – a rehearsal anticipating his arrival here. I know he will be beautiful. Happy. Loved. He will be the most important person in this family. The experts, Kate and Mrs Blainey, tell me that our little darling is definitely a boy. It seems I am the right size for a BIG baby boy.

If you were here right now, you'd know that your friend, Martin Blainey, has come home. His life is a Hell of pain. He is angry. He is dysfunctional. He lives his life in a turmoil of despair.

In spite of my longing to hold you near to me, I give thanks that you are no longer suffering.

I just heard the door latch. Must go and put the kettle on.

Goodnight, my darling.

2

Caitlin

Three bodies filled the hallway and three voices talked over each other. It was impossible to know who was saying what. I heard, 'What a great…voice…loved that last song…wish Caitlin…my that was a long walk…' Their chatter brought the house to life once more.

Kate led the way into the kitchen and for the next hour all four of us sat around the table drinking pots of tea and munching on sourdough scones.

'Imagine, Caitlin,' Kate announced. 'They raised £457. Indeed now, that'll be a lovely boost for the veterans fund.'

'And I won the draw,' Molly said, plonking a small basket on the table.

'Now, Molly, I'm thinkin' that we should give that to our good neighbour. It'll brighten up her life a little bit so it will.'

'That's just what I was thinking, Ma. I'll take it to her tomorrow.'

When I asked Bridie if she enjoyed the concert, she became very still.

'Indeed I did, Caitlin. The songs were Patrick's songs, but the voices were not as pure and rich as Pat's. He was sorely missed. We missed you too, Caitlin, but sure enough you were wise to stay home.'

All nodded agreement and as I looked at three flushed faces, I understood a good measure of love sat safely in their hearts for me.

The centre of our world had collapsed and each corner of our existence had become a challenge for survival. Bridie poured her grief into scrubbing floors, leaving buckets and mops and dusters around as she moved her attention from one job to another. Although the dining room table and dresser rarely got used these days, she polished and buffed every square inch of wood until she could no longer see through her tear-stained eyes. Then, she'd just sit and stare into space. Patrick's death had silenced Molly. She no longer made life noisy for people around her. She no longer thumped heels as she walked, or slammed cupboard doors. Now, it was as if she walked with only air beneath her feet, and cupboard doors became fragile in her hands. Her sadness manifested in cakes and bread baked in silent simmering anger.

Kate admonished, 'Now, Molly, if you don't put love into your baking, it'll turn out twisted and not worthy of our table.'

And so, our fractured shapeless days carried us forward.

3

Harry

Harry Kenihan had a lot on his mind lately and his mother, Lettie, couldn't speer the who, the why and the how of it. She'd invited a few of the local lassies to share a meal with them in the hope that he'd become interested. Harry welcomed them with smiles and offered drinks. He made sure their guests were comfortably attended to but that was as much as he could offer. These attempts at matchmaking left Lettie's face stamped with a perpetual bewildered question mark.

Earlier that morning when Harry was leaving for work, she'd lectured him. 'You're spendin' too much time alone, Harry.'

'I'm fine, Ma, don't you be worrying about me. See ye later.' He patted Bonza, the border collie, jumped on his motorbike and whizzed off to the *Numurkah Leader* office.

'See, Bonza, did ye hear that?' Lettie whispered, 'In the auld days, he'd be whistling wi' happiness at times like this.'

When Harry reached the corner where Broken Creek turned west, he stopped and dismounted. He walked over and sat under a giant peppercorn tree. Its branches stretched halfway across the river and dominated the muddy banks.

'Strewth! Look at the size o' you. I remember when you were only six feet tall, barely strong enough to support a couple of wild hellions on a rope swing.'

As if the tree heard him, the branches swayed gently and shed a few peppercorns.

Over the slap and slide of the river, Harry heard footsteps behind him.

'Talkin' to yersel, Harry eh? What's up?' Dave, a workmate, sat down next to Harry. He hugged his knees. 'Girl trouble?'

'Nope…well, you could say that, Dave. It's just that since I got back from France, my mother has been engineering romances for me. First it was Kathleen, her helper. Ma managed to have her hanging around when I came home from work. When I said I wasn't interested, she lamented, "Well, Harry, ye did say you'd consider asking her oot, didn't ye? An' it's been months sin ye said that. I thocht I'd gie ye time tae adjust. Whit's wrang wi' the lassie that ye don't want tae take her oot?"'

Dave keeled over laughing.

'I told her, nothing's wrong wi' her, Ma, she's a nice girl. But she's no' for me. I don't want ye doin' any matchmakin', I'll do my own when I'm good and ready. She took notice of what I'd said for a month or so until Fiona, the daughter of her Scottish friend Mrs Campbell, appeared on the scene. She said then, "She's a nice wee lassie, Harry, an' you'll baith unerstaun the language."'

Dave chortled, 'Mothers are like that, Harry, an' you've gone all bloody Scottish on me. Didn't know ye were bilingual.'

'I know that fine an' she is my ma but I don't want her interferin' in my life. When I told her that, she got real titchy. She glared at me sayin, "Well, don't lose the rag wi' me, Harry, I just want ye tae be sharin' your life wi' some decent young woman. It's no' right that ye don't have a good woman tae spend yer life wi." That mornin' when I made for the door, I told her, "Leave me be, Ma, I'm happy in my own company." She sulked for days after that. The thing is, Dave, ever since getting a letter with the news that my Irish mate from Langley died, I can't get the idea out o' my head that his lovely wife Caitlin is now on her own. She's a real beauty. That's no' to say Aussie girls aren't but I keep seein' fair English skin and a gorgeous face. An' such a smile – it lights up a room like no other. When she smiled at me during the days I'd spent with Paddy and his family, it was like receiving a gift. Don't know what I'll do with this feeling…maybe I'll write to her…see how she's doin'. Now she's waiting for the sproggy to arrive, she might like a letter from the antipodes to cheer her up. Ma's been knitting something for Paddy's youngster. Think I'll send a note wi' that.'

'Sounds like a bloody good idea, Harry. Tell your mother. Might give her something else to worry about.' He laughed and stood up. 'Gotta go, Harry. Good luck.'

4

Caitlin

When Patrick's Australian friend, Harry Kenihan, had spent Christmas 1918 with us, he'd sat with us around the dining room table making paperchains with pages cut from magazines. He helped to decorate the parlour. We sang 'Away in a Manger' and 'Silent Night' while cutting and glueing. We laughed about Christmas traditions and funny individual stories about our most embarrassing moments. He showed us how to make what he called 'damper' and he'd managed to get Patrick out to the local tavern, where the sound of his laughter, through gasps for breath, had given us false hope for his recovery. It was a happy hiatus.

I'd written to Harry and sent him the souvenirs Pat had packed up for him. I also told him the good news about our expected baby. I didn't expect a reply, but a week before the baby was born I received a brown paper parcel tied tight with red twine, sealed with wax and showing colourful Australian stamps. I had to cut through four layers of thick paper to get to the contents…the most beautiful circular knitted shawl of filigree lace. A note from Harry's mother, pinned to the shawl, expressed sympathy along with good wishes for the health of the baby and me.

Harry wrote,

Dear Caitlin

Thanks for sending the balaclava and tin from Paddy. I'll figure out what to do with them later. I'm wondering; how are you faring? I would like to know when the baby arrives and how you both are. Since I got home, life in Numurkah has been a bit up and down but I'm back working at my old job in the newspaper office and getting to like it. My ma sends her regards.

All the best,

Harry

*

Langley, Berks

7 March 1920

Dear Mrs Kenihan

What a beautiful gift. I love the intricate work and will treasure it always. It won't be long now until my baby is wrapped in the warmth of your good wishes. He (or she) will be the best-dressed baby in the village. Please know that your kindness is very much appreciated. I am so pleased that Harry arrived home safely. I'm sure he will brighten up your life, as he did ours not so long ago.

Wishing you good health,

Caitlin O'Hare

*

I enclosed a note to Harry expressing appreciation of his company at the end of the war, and how he'd cheered us up with his banter and humour. I reminded him of the fun we'd had when he recited Paterson's poem. I could almost reach out and touch the faces, and hear the laughter that accompanied the memory.

5

Caitlin

On most evenings while waiting for this brand-new person to arrive, Molly, Bridie and I settled in the parlour surrounded by paper patterns; swaths of white cotton; knitting needles and wool. I pinned the tissue paper to fabric, and Bridie cut around the outline. Molly basted the pieces together and all three of us stitched tiny nightgowns and wraps with satin ties that would keep the baby secure and warm.

I asked, 'Why does everyone think this baby is a boy?'

'Of course it's a boy,' Molly piped up. 'Look at the shape o' you.'

'What d'you mean? What shape? Aren't I supposed to be this shape?'

'Indeed you are, but Mrs Blainey said you're the shape of a boy.'

Bridie put in her tuppence worth. 'I don't know how she's worked that out but I just hope St Gerard stays close to Caitlin, and the baby will come through this all right. Boy or girl, they'll be a blessing to this house so they will.'

Molly recorded our predictions about weight, date of arrival and gender.

When things grew quiet or late, I climbed the stairs to the room I'd shared with my man. I refused kind offers of help to sort out his personal belongings and on nights when loneliness kept me awake, I looked through his clothes to recapture the scent of his body. It puzzled me that you can still smell an entity through shirts and coats they had worn long ago but the form refuses to manifest. Also, I found it strange that when I saw Patrick in my mind's eye, he was the young healthy, whole Patrick from before the war. At these times, I wrapped myself in his clothing and wept while my faith in a benevolent God fizzled and died.

After selecting a few of his favourite books to keep for myself, I gave volumes to Martin Blainey. Molly's fiancé, Michael, suggested I send some to the British Legion, where veterans gathered to drink beer and swap lies about women they'd met in the war.

The remainder was put in boxes, and I turned my attention to a trunk full of papers, letters and diaries Patrick had kept over the years. On silent nights, the rustle of handwritten pages told me truths I'd never dreamed of. Truths about the desecration of young men, destruction of French farmsteads and mud that clung to your clothes like a bad smell. In a copy of Yeats's poetry, I found a letter addressed to me. For some reason, Patrick had never mailed it.

France, Spring 1917

My Dear Caitlin

When I come home from this Hell, I will ask you to marry me. We will honeymoon in the most beautiful wooded valley in Ireland. We will walk beside the Avonmore River, a lovely wide river with deep pools that flow through areas of mountain blanket bog. We will gather some of the rare orchids that bloom on its banks and scan the sky for a peregrine falcon diving to clutch a rabbit or moorhen in its talons. We will wander from the foothills of the South Dublin Mountains through the glens of Glendalough to the dramatic mountains of Aghavannagh. On an early morning we will drive to the beaches of Brittas Bay and skip stones for fun. We will buy a kiln-fired bowl showing all the colours of the valley and I will sing to you:

> There is not in this wide world a valley so sweet,
> as the vale in whose bosom the wide waters meet.
> ere the last rays of summer and life does depart,
> the bloom of this valley shall stay in my heart...

I closed my eyes. I'd heard him sing this song and it seemed to me that echoes of his voice filled the air where I sat. On his return from France, Patrick carried a notebook. He'd written notes to me asking questions about homecomings; reviews about new shows and plays in the West End; new poetry by authors like May Wedderburn and Siegfried Sassoon. The musical comedy *Chu Chin Chow* at Her Majesty's Theatre had been running since August 1916 and we'd promised ourselves we'd see it when Pat came home, but we never did.

In the beginning of Pat's repatriation, he'd stood away from me like he couldn't bear to be seen by my eyes. His sisters and mother were allowed to tend to him but not me. His mother said things like, 'I don't like the look of him today.' Or, 'He's a sorry sight,' when talking about him.

To Pat she'd say, 'Dth dth, Pat, don't turn your back on Caitlin now. She's a sight for sore eyes now, isn't she?'

At one of these times, I remember, he stood stock still for a long moment looking at his feet. Back then, I understood that my lover of before the war still hid behind the reality of his pain. The anguish of knowing this at times made me want to weep enough to raise the levels of the sea so that everywhere there'd be water to heal, to soothe the universal pain away, and all the beautiful young men would laugh and sing with the energy of their ages and all the severed parts would be rejoined. But Patrick's recurring nightmares whizzed and whooshed across the mire and immovable images of young dead men lying in mud. During his visit, Harry Kenihan had understood that Pat was dealing with these nightmares. It was as if for a little while, the sun shone in our house banishing the darkness like a light switching on.

6

Harry

Numurkah

March 1920

Hello, Caitlin

This is my third try at writing to you. I hope I'm not intruding into your life.

When I started this letter, I was standing under a gum tree, until I heard raindrops spitting on the leaves above me. I made a dash for home before my words got washed away like the dust on my boots. Water lashed all around me. Water obliterated the road in places, just like it did the last time I saw England. I nearly missed the turn to home I got to thinking about Paddy and you and hoping you are hunky-dory, what with the baby due and all. I'm sure with all the care you're getting, you'll be beaming with good health. I can't add 'happiness' — your emotions at this time will be seesawing with the passing hours.

The rain has stopped and the sun has blessed the bushes, making them sparkle like tiny fairy lights. So now, I'm off to post this and have a long turn on my motorbike.

Hoping to hear some good news from you real soon.

Good luck,

    Harry Kenihan

7

Caitlin

Patrick Joseph James O'Hare decided to greet the world on 17 March. Snow driven by blustery winds scurried into tree trunks and cabbages and amongst the snowdrops popping up along the edges of lawn. It floated onto the vegetable garden. It lay on top of the brick wall at the end of the garden like layers of goose down and by the evening of that day the roads had become impassable. The temperature dropped, hardening the snow on the pathways into solid ice to make walking hazardous.

A few weeks earlier, at Kate's insistence, the phone had been installed but on that night, connections to the outside world were cut. By the time Molly set out for the local midwife's house two streets away, I was sure the baby would drop at my feet. I walked up and down the hallway with Bridie beside me massaging my back.

Kate knelt and prayed. 'O Holy St Gerard, help this child into the world…and while you're in a favourable mood, get a message to the doctor…blessed Mary, mother o' God, help Caitlin.' She repeated her supplications without taking a breath.

Bridie and I giggled as we staggered.

Everything we needed for the birth was set up in the downstairs parlour and it seemed to me that Pat's family was expecting triplets with the piles of towels, linen, basins and candles stacked on every surface. We heard the door open and close, then footsteps in the lobby.

'Was on a call down the street,' Doctor Kinloch said, pulling off his gloves, scarf and hat and turning his back to the fire.

'Thank you,' Kate shouted to the ceiling, clapping her hands and struggling to her feet.

An hour later, the doctor held the baby up and I shrieked with fright. His face had no features. None at all. 'Patrick! Patrick!' I screamed.

Kate came to my side and held her hands in front of my face. 'Caitlin…breath easy now…breath easy now,' she coaxed.

'What's all the yellin' about now, woman. Haven't ye never seen a babby born wit' a caul?' Doctor Kinloch laid my son down on the bed at my feet and with his two thumbs under the baby's chin, he rolled a film of thin, pink skin up over the tiny face. And there, screaming lustily at last, was the most beautiful being I'd ever seen.

Kate bathed him. Bridie dressed him. First in a tiny vest, nappy and barracoat. Next came a white cotton nightgown showing rows of blue embroidered violets on the cuffs and the frilly bottom edge. The final layer was the beautiful Australian shawl from Mrs Kenihan. At last he was handed to me. I took one look at my darling and forgave him everything.

Molly returned with the midwife and, after the initial excitement and chattering subsided, we decided he would be known as Joseph. He wriggled approval in my arms.

'No need of your skills now,' Kinloch said to the midwife.

She shrugged, 'Hmph,' and glared at him. 'I'll stay and make my acquaintance with this lovely new soul so I will.'

Kate poured herself and the doctor a good measure of whisky. 'It's a grand job you've done this night, doctor, God bless ye.' Then she dipped her finger in her glass and blessed Joseph on the top of his head.

Later, while I enjoyed a cup of tea, Kate sat in the chair she'd rocked her own son in and sang an ancient ditty to his son:

> 'Ali bali ali bali bee
> Sittin' on your granny's knee
> Waitin' for a wee bawbee
> Tae buy some Coulter's candy.'

With Joseph's birth, I learned what it was to be bound heart to heart with another human being. This knowledge came with a minute measure of resentment. I missed his father so much, I could hardly look at my son without understanding the true meaning of bittersweet. I confided my feelings to Bridie.

'Oh well, Caitlin. Tis understood that ye loved Pat and you're missin' him. But surely it won't be long at all until you'll find a greater measure o' love in your wee darlin' here. Look at him now. Isn't he just a miracle?'

When Joseph was newly born, Kate dished out advice to me with cups of strong tea and plates piled high with her delicious applecake. 'Now m'dear,' she'd say, stroking the baby's head, 'never show a babby in a looking glass before they're a year old, it isn't good for their soul so it isn't.' And another: 'Never cut their tiny fingernails with scissors. If they get raggedy, ye soften the edges wi' your own saliva.'

I only half listened to her. I was too busy staring at two beautiful Kerry blue eyes and a mop of jet-black curls.

8

Caitlin

Langley, Berks
25 March 1920

Dear Harry

This is to let you know that Patrick Joseph James O'Hare arrived on 17 March. We named him after his father and my father. He will be known as Joseph and we are all sure that Patrick would approve the choice. How appropriate that he chose the feast day of Ireland's patron saint to come in to the world. His grandmother is ecstatic about it, as Pat would have been. He looks very much like Pat. Dark curly hair and the bluest of eyes. He hasn't yet learned the difference between day and night but we're working on that together. He and I are both being treated like royalty by Bridie, Molly and especially Kate. I'm intrigued by the name of your town and wonder about the size and shape of it. One day I want to tell young Joseph about the place his shawl came from.

Best wishes,
Caitlin O'Hare

9

Caitlin

While I'd sat with Pat's mother during his dying days, one of the most disturbing things was that the baby would never hear his father singing and we'd never share the birth of our child. I told Kate then that I'd always and ever hold Pat's songs in my heart.

She responded, 'Och, Caitlin, it's glad I am to hear you say that. Now tell me again about a time when you and Pat walked out together.'

Then she'd sit back in her chair, close her eyes and let her lips smile at my stories: the summer evenings when Pat and I strolled with friends, or each other, along the riverbank or country lanes burgeoned with summer blossoms and how we'd laughed and touched and dreamt of a future. Funny and strange how, back then, I was never quite able to see us in years to come.

Once, when the world was full of colour – blue, lilac, pink and red crocuses; it must have been spring – I remember feeling cold and then the warmth of Pat's jacket as he draped it around my shoulders. We were walking in late afternoon. The light faded. The flowers were closing their petals for the end of their day's brilliance. Our friendship strengthened and grew sturdy through the simplicity of those gestures and times. They were the foundation that we built the edifice of us upon. I couldn't quite conjure up what shape the days and years would take beyond 1916. Never ever did I see myself in widowhood with Patrick dead and cold as the marble that marked his grave. Argh, those outings and evenings – killed stone dead.

Reunion

Last night I dreamt
That you had come back to us
I saw your shining face
and heard your soft-song voice.
Our joyous tears mingled.
We laughed and sang
five-voice muted melodies.
Last night I dreamt.

10

Harry

Numurkah

2 May 1920

Dear Caitlin

Great news about the new arrival – glad to hear that you're being well looked after.

About Numurkah: population 1,200 if we count the boys who never came back. The town sits nicely in north-western Victoria – precisely, north of Tallygaroopna, west of Katamatite and east of Waaia. (That's a lesson on pronunciation for you and young Joseph.)

The town is mainly a service town for rural fruit growers in the shire. There are two general stores, a newspaper office (where I work), four hotels and, best of all, House Bros Foundry. My best pal, Danny Coffey, and I used to look in the open doors, fascinated by the blaze of light, the roaring heat and the noise of the anvils. Every day at twelve o'clock, the foundry whistle blows. It can be heard everywhere in town. That's the time of day when I miss Danny the most. Or maybe it's when I sit down by the creek and remember the adventures we had there. Or maybe it's… I know you'll get the picture.

The thing I like about Numurkah is that everyone has room to move. Houses are built on big blocks and the streets are wide enough for all the horse-drawn traffic that needs it. Now that cars are becoming a faster mode of transport, there's many a runaway horse scared of the engine noise. Maybe one day you'll see it for yourself.

The thing I don't like about it is that Danny didn't make it back from France. Shellfire hit him. I found his body in bits. His mother arrived at our door a while back, with Danny's dog. She wanted me to have him. His name's Bonza. Now, every time I see Mrs Coffey, I never know what to say to her. I'd love to be able to take the stamp of sadness away from her face.

My mother says, 'All the best to Caitlin and the bairn.' I would like to hear from you again. Soon. Cheerio for now,

Your friend,

Harry Kenihan

11

Caitlin

Langley, Berks
20 June 1920

Dear Harry

Thank you for your last letter. There has been a lot happening here. Firstly, though, Joseph and I are both well. He's thriving. In the words of Granny Kate, 'Sure it's a wonder to watch. He's shooting up like the leeks in the vegetable garden so he is.'

Thank you for the information about Numurkah, although pronouncing the place names had my tongue in a knot. Living somewhere with wide, wide roads and lots of space is a lot different from here. As you know, the streets are barely wide enough to allow two carts to pass each other. To satisfy my curiosity, I'd like to know how you spend your days in your widespread land. What kind of work do you do at the newspaper office? Who are your friends?

The next big news: Molly and Michael are getting married in August and are planning to live in Oxford. Michael has been tenured to the history faculty at the university there and Molly has found permanent work with the Red Cross rehabilitating returned servicemen. The biggest change in our lives is that Kate and Bridie are planning to go and live in Ireland. Kate often threatened to do this, so it wasn't too much of a surprise. They'll be sorely missed. Especially by Joseph – he already adores them. It will be strangely quiet without the tribes of visitors that Kate attracts. My concern is the continual fight for Ireland's independence and how Kate and Bridie will cope with it all.

I do hope you are well and enjoying your work. Give my regards to your mother and thank her again for the beautiful shawl.

Best wishes,

Caitlin

12

Harry

Numurkah
10 August 1920

Dear Caitlin

Your last letter is very much appreciated. Great stuff! My ma says hello to you and the wean – she wants to know if he's babbling baby noises yet. Knowing his birthright, I'd say he's chattering away at a mile a minute. I am pleased that you're both well.

You asked how I spend my days. Well, it's pretty routine here. First thing in the morning, before I head off to work, if it hasn't rained for a few days, I water the garden and maybe do a bit of weeding or pruning. Ma thinks this is great: it lets her get on with her sewing jobs – that is, after she's cooked my breakfast. I'm getting used to the wonder of home-cooked meals, like bacon and eggs and Ma's potato scones. I still remember that wonderful Christmas feast at your place in 1918. It was a real lifesaver for me. Remember the fun we had with the tokens in the pudding? I still have the silver threepenny bit that I won. I think it was Bridie who got the thimble – she was annoyed because she really wanted the ring.

My work at the newspaper means writing articles about the local community. Like successes in sport or where the next farm auction will be held or what dignitaries are attending important events – nothing too exciting happens in Numurkah these days. I do an odd spread on how the war veterans and their families are faring. This gives me opportunities to keep in touch with them and I like that. My boss is pleased with my work. He thinks I should do a formal course in journalism but that might mean a temporary shift to Melbourne. I'm not quite ready for that yet but it's something to think about.

Bonza and I go out bush at times on my motorbike. He's a long-haired border collie, black with white paws and white blaze on his chest. He sits in a cardboard box labelled 'Eggs' tied tight to the front of my seat, and I'm sure he laughs when the wind runs through his coat. So there you are, Caitlin, not much to write about, but life is good. It would be just great if we could keep up this letter writing. I can hear your voice in the ink. Look after yourself now.

All the best,

Harry

13

Caitlin

On a hot Saturday morning in August 1920, Molly exchanged wedding vows with Michael O'Meara. Molly had designed and made her ivory silk wedding dress. It reached to just below her knees and showed off white stockings and button-down shiny white shoes. Her hair was held in place by a filmy lace cap that edged the line of her eyebrows. A family heirloom of a short christening veil, pinned to the cap at the nape of her neck, swung loosely at her back. Instead of a bouquet, she clutched a Catholic missal, a gift from her Aunt Maeve in Ireland. A corsage of carnations decorated the mother-of-pearl front cover. Molly's face shone enough to light up the church and embrace everyone there.

The full nuptial mass took an hour and a half. The new young priest who conducted the ceremony talked to the congregation about hope for the future and conferred a papal blessing on the happy pair. For this wedding, the choir sang and the bells peeled. Bridie was the only bridesmaid. She wore the same dove-grey outfit she'd dressed in when Pat and I were married just over a year before. Michael stood tall and straight until the part where he put the ring on Molly's finger. Then he bent close to her, took her hand gently, looked into her eyes and anyone could see his adoration. A moment of envy brought tears to my eyes.

A reception had been organised in the church hall and for a while it was as if there had been a collective vow to forget about the damages the war had wrought on this community. This was an event for enjoying the music and food and company as a respite from the shared grief.

When Michael and Molly took to the floor for the bridal waltz, a lump as big as a cricket ball rose in my throat. I made the excuse that my baby needed a drink and carried him to the anteroom. Kate followed. The two of us had a quiet crying session.

Kate took my hand and cuddled Joseph in her arms. 'Go on back, m'dear, have a wee dance wi' the groom. It's a long time dead we are, and God knows you can surely use a bit of lightness in your life. I know Pat wouldn't mind at all if you shared Molly and Michael's happiness.'

I hugged her and scooted out to the gathering. Someone hauled me on to the floor for the 'Brown Jug Polka'. Then I was partnered to a young schoolboy who trailed me through the steps of the 'Siege of Ennis'. I fell exhausted and deliriously happy onto the first available chair, and the music settled to sedate waltzes.

Michael's brother, Anthony, read from telegrams sent by a few people who were unable to attend: 'May you see your children's children. May you be poor in misfortune and rich in blessing. May you know nothing but happiness from this day forward. A wise man once said, 'I don't know the answer – ask a woman.'

I found myself laughing hilariously with the other guests at the witticisms. Sadly, this is the part when Patrick would honour and entertain the company with songs and funny stories. I thought I felt his hand on my shoulder like a tender touch of approval.

Just then, Michael stood up and put a hand on Molly's shoulder. 'Now did you hear about the two bed bugs…they got married in the spring!' While people were still chortling, 'Now for the serious bit. Molly and I will be leaving this lovely place and you, the loveliest of friends and family. It appears that the buildings and halls of learning at Oxford, require my presence. I am honoured to tell you that I'm here today also as proxy to our dear Patrick. Before he died, Patrick wrote the following words for us: "May you never lie, steal, cheat or drink. But if you must steal, then steal away my sorrows. And if you must lie,

lie with each other all the nights of your life. And if you must cheat, then please cheat death…because you couldn't live without each other. And if you must drink, drink in the moments that take your breath away."'

Silence. Feet shuffling. Sobs. Then the wail of a fiddle from a corner of the stage and someone began a chorus of 'Whisky in the Jar' and sadness got lost in the words. I sat stunned.

Later that day, the delirious pair was farewelled amongst clouds of rose petals thrown by laughing guests. Some settled on Molly's head and Michael gently brushed them off as they moved through the crowd to a waiting cab. They were like two lovers escaping from home, running away with radiant hearts. Kate had made a white lacy horseshoe with the intention that Joseph would present it to them but when the moment came, he refused to relinquish it. In the end, I had to pry his fingers loose from it and people got a laugh when they saw that it was wet and sticky from his sucking on it.

Kisses and hugs were many and genuine. The charabanc was decorated with old shoes, tin cans, and great bunches of flowers.

Molly called out, 'I'll write and hope that you will too.'

Michael held the cab door open for her, then reached into a side pocket of his jacket, and threw a handful of coins into the crowd. The bride and groom were ignored by the younger guests as they madly scrambled to get to the sixpences, silver threepenny bits and a rare shilling.

14

Caitlin

For Joseph's first birthday, the roads were clear, the sun shone and snowdrops and bluebells heralded spring. He had no idea what the fuss was about. He was blissfully unaware that he'd reached the important stage of being one year old.

Bridie had dressed him in a white satin romper suit that would've fitted a three-year-old and he clawed at the bow tie under his chubby chin. 'He'll grow into it, Caitlin,' she whispered while I turned up the cuffs.

'But you can't even see his knees, Bridie. It won't fit him for another two years! And see, he's tugging at the tie. He doesn't like it at all.'

Just then Kate appeared at the bedroom door and Joseph shouted, 'Gamma,' and fled to her side as fast as his chubby little legs could go. He grabbed the edge of her skirt and said again, 'Gamma!'

Kate held both his hands and stood him apart from her. 'In the name o' Saint Jude, what are you two doin' tae the darlin' boy? That suit won't do at all. This is to be a day o' fun – now how can Joseph enjoy eatin' ice cream and jelly in that dress-up?'

Bridie and I shrugged and looked at our feet. Kate's eyes twinkled with mirth and all three adults burst into laughter. Joseph looked from one to the other, clapped his hands and chortled with us.

Mrs Blainey, from next door, arrived carrying a parcel that turned out to be a toy drum. Joseph's beaming smile assured her that she had chosen well and he spent the next while learning how to get the loudest noise from it. A few neighbour children and their mothers arrived with gifts.

Bridie announced a game of the Grand Old Duke of York. Loud shouts from the children, sighs from the adults, Kate bashing the tune and singing full force. The clamour of trying to get children into formation challenged Bridie's patience. Besides, Joseph was only interested in beating the loudest possible racket from his new toy.

Bridie gave up in frustration and put the kettle on. A pot of tea was very much needed. By the end of the afternoon, Joseph could've started his very own one-man band. Two flutes, a xylophone, drums and harmonica needed little skill in getting a noise out of them. When the cake was crumbs on a platter and the ice cream drizzle on bowls, the visiting mothers sighed with relief. They whispered goodbye and guided their charges to the door. Bridie stacked dishes on the kitchen bench. Joseph slid under the dining room table and fell asleep with the drumsticks glued to his sticky little fingers.

15

Caitlin

Langley, Berks
25 March 1921

Dear Harry

Thank you for your last letter. I enjoyed reading about your work at the newspaper. I'm sure it keeps you very busy and interested in the life of your town.

Joseph's first birthday was chaotic. Neighbours arrived with noise-making toys and he had a lovely time – tearing wrapping from each package. I wasn't sure how he would feel when he woke – too many choices of rich food for one so young. No matter how much I protested about it, I was outnumbered. Result was, he was sick during the night. I'm thinking that today both he and I will subsist on only bread and water.

There are more whispers about Kate going to live in Ireland. I think she's having a difficult time telling me about it but one of these days I'm sure she will blurt it out. Maybe I should pour her a double measure of whisky. Not that she usually needs that to loosen her tongue, but making her plans public seems to be causing her concern. By the time I write to you again, I will know more.

I enjoy your letters and would be very happy to keep up our correspondence. Meanwhile, Harry, keep well and keep busy. That's the best road to a happy life.

Your friend,

Caitlin

16

Nina

Nina Grottenthaler stood in front of a mirror in her bedroom. She pulled softly at a strand of dry lifeless hair that had long since lost its lustre. Since learning about her son Karl's death, grief had stung her soul to profound sadness. From the edge of her eyes to each side of her mouth, furrows of flesh looked like they'd been gouged with a blunt blade. An expression of perplexed despair settled on her face like a reflection of her country's devastation from the terms of the Versailles Treaty. Tears had washed the blue from her eyes and faded them to a milky shadow of the past. Instead of bathing and dressing each morning, Nina now spent time facing her dead son's photo.

Before the war, she'd found contentment in a patch of garden at the back of her house. An adjoining chicken coop she shared with an ageing neighbour had kept both supplied with eggs of precious protein. Due to neglect, the fecundity of her garden had flown. Now, chicken carcasses lay amongst the weeds that choked the cabbages and leeks and carrots – all gone to seed.

Late in 1919, Nina had received in her mail a small package with English stamps. It contained letters, photographs and a rosary that Karl had on him when he died. Each item was wrapped separately in delicate silk fabric as if the sender had considered them to be sanctified. A short two-line message had no signature or returning address. She'd placed the rosary on top of the letter. Most days she'd wrap herself in a feather quilt and after kissing the beads, she'd chant the ritual of the rosary. *Ave Maria gratsia plena. Pater nostra. In unum dei…*the words repeated over and over again until her throat and eyes dried up. Then she'd close her eyes and sleep. The days and nights ran into each other in an endless repetition of prayerful pleading and weeping.

Then, on a day in February 1921, she received a second piece of mail from someone named Harry in Australia. It was a small tobacco tin containing two leave passes and a photo of Karl's friend Inge. Realisation that two kind strangers had known Karl brought a flicker of interest to Nina. Eventually, a semblance of the energy she'd once had, combined with her innate German discipline, forced her into action. She scanned the English words and tried to decipher them but all she learned was the name 'Harry' at the end. Nina began to think of the country where they'd originated.

Later that day, she wrapped herself up in her ten-year-old padded winter coat and walked half a kilometre in the snow to the public library. Before the war, the local council kept these pathways cleared. But now, each person was responsible for shovelling the snow outside their own dwellings.

She plodded. She sagged. She struggled on with hunched shoulders mirroring the mood of the nation. When she noticed that a youngish blond man had replaced the regular librarian, she hesitated by the door.

He smiled and looked straight into her eyes. 'Come in,' he mouthed and put an index finger to his lips.

It turned out that his name was William. Born of a German father and English mother, he was fluent in both languages. Nina gave him the letters and asked if he'd translate them for her. William read the Australian letter, dipped a pen in the inkwell at the corner of his desk. The transcription of the short note took only a minute. Then he asked Nina if she'd like to hear the words in English.

'*Ja, das wäre sehr gut. Danke,*' Nina whispered.

William pointed to a chair in a corner near a heater. She took off her coat so that she could enjoy the warmth. And from this simple conversation, a journey began.

17

Caitlin

After Patrick died, Kate would sometimes sigh and say, 'One day I'm going home to Rathdrum and never coming back here. The smell of peat and heather is in me bones so it is.'

Bridie and I treated these announcements as one of her fantasies until we noticed a stream of letters with Irish postmarks arriving. She didn't share them with us as she usually did. Then one evening, while we listened to Radio Eiren, she revealed that she'd made arrangements to go home.

The next morning over breakfast, Bridie announced, 'Auntie Maeve lives alone and needs looking after and Ma will soon need help, so I'm going too. There's nothing I'd rather do than go to Ireland.'

I'd read about Terence McSwiney's death and his agonising hunger strike, only months ago. 'It seems to me that Ireland is in a bad state right now. How will you deal with the troubles that are besetting the ould sod?'

Kate refused to discuss this. Each time I brought up the subject, she'd say, 'Now, Caitlin, let's be thinking about life and love. Leave the darkness to them that nurture it.'

Letters from Maeve were full of anger and hatred. According to her, the English people were 'a plague of moral lepers'.

'Will you answer that, Kate?'

'I won't. Ye see, Caitlin, Maeve has had to deal with the deaths of more than a few young men. She's very friendly with Muriel McSwiney, who feeds her hostile enmity with the soda bread she brings. Mrs

McSwiney has a powerful mastery of IRA preaching and Maeve listens. My thoughts about all that are beyond the reach of malice.'

'But why would you want to live in that environment? Surely that would trouble you.'

'She's my sister, my own blood, and 'tis surely my place beside her, to help push the hatred away and fill her heart with memories of the times when stories were told and songs were sung and the guns were silent as the grave. It's a beautiful thing to wander into the past and find yourself amongst those that lived. Besides, Caitlin, there's a longing in me to sit by a turf fire and spend what's left of my life amongst the green of my homeland, poor and fractured as it may be. Dhat is the wishes o' my heart and soul. So let's make decisions about what to pack.'

The following days were spent dividing up special pieces of china, furniture and wall hangings between Bridie, Molly, Joseph and me.

'Caitlin, would you now go upstairs to that long press next to your room. You'll see an ould case. Humph it down here and we'll have a look at what's in it so we will.'

A battered dust-covered suitcase was lugged down stairs to the kitchen.

'In here are some t'ings from Patrick's early schooldays. It would be just grand if you found a keepsake or two for the young spalpeen here, wouldn't it now?'

She nodded towards Joseph, who was busily building a strange structure with chairs and floor mats. He hummed quietly as he worked.

The clasps on the suitcase were rusted and difficult to open but with Bridie wielding a trusty screwdriver, access was gained. Amongst swaths of loose papers we found a parcel of children's books. I selected *The Frog Prince* by Walter Crane and *An Old-Fashioned Alphabet Book* by Randolph Caldecott. Patrick's large, juvenile handwriting filled pages with notes about school activities. My heart lurched as I followed the forms of his childish words. Kate and Bridie reminisced about Patrick's stoic efforts to master written forms of both Irish and English languages.

Bridie said, 'Remember, Ma, how he'd read each word aloud whether anyone was listening or not? And when he learned a new word, he'd use it in every sentence until the next new one. Remember when he was about seven years old, at religious instruction; he learned the word "litany". He said, "I like the word litany. It sounds soft like the touch of my tongue on my palate."'

'Yes, 'tis sure enough, Bridie, I remember when "palate" was his favourite word. That was the happiest time of my day. He'd bounce in the door like a football under its own steam, and he'd start reciting the day's learning. He loved every minute of school so he did.'

'Except for sports, Ma. He hated hurling. He only carried the football so people would think he played sport.'

Suddenly, as if a pulse from some unknown power punched my brain, I realised the enormity of the trust that had been placed in me. The scrawls in this suitcase were a legacy for Joseph, and I am the caretaker of that endowment. An indefinable weight threatened to flatten my spirit. Then I turned my head to my son. My life.

18

Caitlin

On a wild March day, roaring winds and lashing rain kept people indoors. After breakfast, Joseph, Bridie and I watched from the front window as the gutters ran full and fast. We watched one brave shopper almost take flight when her umbrella turned inside out to become a dangerous missile. She skittered across the pathway holding on to the handle with both hands while her shopping bag swung from the crook of one elbow. We saw her mouth open wide in what looked like a cry for help before the weapon slipped from her hands and whooshed across the road. It got entangled in the garden hedge of the house opposite like a drunken warrior.

'Oh my!' Bridie shouted, leaping to her feet. 'It's Mrs Blainey! Poor thing's drenched. I'll be back in a jiffy.' She grabbed a mac from the hallstand and raced to help our neighbour.

Kate joined us at the window. 'As if Agnes hadn't enough trouble in her life. Put the kettle on, Caitlin. I'm thinkin' she'll want a hot drink.'

Bridie almost carried her charge up the path and in through the front door. Within a few minutes, Kate and Agnes were ensconced by the fire, interrupting each other with exclamations about the weather and the price of tea.

Mrs Blainey said, 'I'll be mournin' the loss o' your good counsel Kate. My heart is sore at your leavin'.'

'Och, away wi' ye, Agnes. Now there's postage stamps and ye can write, so we'll be in touch.'

'I know that, Kate, but I doubt if a pot o' your lovely tea would survive the shooglin' o' the ferry.'

Their laughter rang long and hearty.

At this point, plans for leaving England were in place and on a bleak April night Kate and Bridie sailed across St Georges Channel to Rosslare.

19

Caitlin

Langley, Berks

1 November 1921

Dear Harry

It has been a while since I wrote to you and all I can say about that is, *mea culpa.*

Kate and Bridie have gone and the house is cavernous without their company, so I thought it a good idea to use the silence to write a few more words in answer to your last letter. I was pleased to read that you have opportunities to keep in touch with grieving families. I'm sure they will appreciate your understanding of their situations. The suggestion of a course in journalism seems exciting – who knows what that would mean for your future? I hope you consider all the angles of moving away from your hometown. When you were here, I remember you showing us photos of you and your friend Danny. He was a fine young man and I understand the heartbreak his death brings to you and to his mother. Next time you see Mrs Coffey, tell her my thoughts are with her.

It's snowing enough outside to build a snowman. Joseph and I are about to have some fun in the nearby park. The Irish streak in him is fighting for independence and his determined struggles with coat buttons and laced-up boots are a sight to see.

Right now, it gives me an opportunity to update you on O'Hare family news. Molly and Michael will be spending three whole days with us over Christmas. It will be an opportunity for Molly and me to reminisce about our time together during the war. Joseph no doubt will be happy to play big brother to baby Isabella, who will be five months old by then. I haven't seen Molly since Isabella was born and I'm looking forward to having their company. Mrs Blainey and Martin will join Joseph and me for breakfast and later in the afternoon, a few of my Red Cross colleagues will arrive.

I can't imagine what it would be like to cook a Christmas feast in the Australian summer heat. My kitchen becomes a furnace with the stove and gas burners on for hours, and this is in midwinter. I do miss Bridie and Kate at this time, not only for their good cooking – for their company. The garlands turned out lopsided – some were too short to reach the full length of the wall. I thought of the Christmas we shared. You were so agile scaling up and down the ladder like a whippet after a runaway rabbit. This year, Joseph and I were more like two sleep-deprived tortoises shuffling and crawling about in wayward links of coloured paper.

We're planning a trip to Ireland. I haven't told him yet because he'd batter my ears with questions about when. And why. And what. And he does enough of that in the normal course of our day. He's tugging at my coat now, so I'll say cheerio and wish you and your mother all the best.

Your friend,
Caitlin

20

Harry

Numurkah
1 February 1922

Dear Caitlin

Two letters in a row from you. Thank you. It is very much appreciated that you took the time. I hope you and your little rug rat had a great time with Molly and Michael. Your life has changed a lot since we were last in each other's company. I hope there's been some good times and that you're making the most of it.

Reading about you having fun in the snow reminds me of a trip that Ma took Danny and me on when we were about twelve years old. We went by bus, train then pony trap for the last leg to the high country. I'd never seen a mountain (or a hill for that matter). Danny and I had the best time chasing each other over snowy heights. We hired skis and swooped and hooped ourselves through gullies and over moguls like a pair of heathens on holiday. Ma was quite happy to sit by a window and make friends in the ski field tearoom.

I can hear her voice saying over and over again, 'I'm happy just tae have a wee walk, set my gaze at these hills and imagine I'm in Scotland. Except as far as I remember, the mountains there are older and blacker. So you boys jist go and have yersels some fun and dinna be breakin' any bones now.'

For as long as I can remember, she'd say, 'Ane day, when I've got mair time, I'm gettin' a giant mechanical shovel an' shape those paddocks o' ours intae the head and shoulders o' Ben Lomond.' That's a mountain in Scotland (you probably know that). She said this to Danny that day on the way back from the high country.

He laughed and said, 'Sure ye will, Mrs Kenihan. We'll help you, eh Harry?'

So thanks, Caitlin, for reminding me of a good time.

Our house was full to bursting on Christmas Day. We have no relatives here but my mother has a widespread network of friends and neighbours. They started arriving around ten o'clock in the morning and the last of them left after ten at night. It got pretty noisy at one point and when some revellers started up with the old Scottish sentimental songs about partings and love and longing, the dog and I took ourselves off out bush for a while. I'm not antisocial, as you know, but I just got to thinking about Danny and your Pat, and so many others who no longer share these festivities.

There are a growing number of cars in the streets of Numurkah. My boss has bought a Model T and he says I can use it occasionally for long-distance assignments. It would be real nice if one day I could take you and wee Joseph on a long trip to see and hear the sights and sounds of Australia.

I appreciate your last letter and understand about your feelings of loneliness. In fact, I know what your face looks like in loneliness. Once, at Christmas '18 when we were hanging paper decorations and Paddy was sitting in a corner of the parlour, I watched you watching him. You looked lonely and I wondered how anyone could feel like that amongst a house full of people. You looked up and saw me. In a fleeting moment, it seemed to me that chemistry mixed our sadnesses and formed a point of recognition between us. Then you smiled and the room returned to yuletime things, but I've never forgotten that split second.

One other thing, Caitlin: I received a letter from Frau Grottenthaler the other day. She thanked me for sending Karl's belongings. Let me know if you'd like me to send it to you. Imagine, she's just one amongst the millions of grieving families in the aftermath of THE GREAT BLOODY WAR.

It's good to read about your next-door neighbour and how you watch out for each other. I'm heartened when I think of the kindness you show to each other. That's so much easier than hatred – don't you think?

That's all for now, Caitlin. I've probably ranted on for long enough. Take good care of yourself.

Your friend,

Harry

21

Caitlin

Langley, Berks
15 April 1922

Dear Harry

Thank you for your February missive. It would be lovely to give whatever ships are carrying your letters a good hard push to get them here quicker.

Firstly, Joseph and I had a lovely time with Molly, Michael and Isabella. As predicted, he played the big brother. Occasional fleeting bouts of jealousy challenged our mothering skills but, overall, he was happy to share his favourite toys and he was generous with hugs and kisses.

The term 'high country' is new to me. Perhaps you could elaborate in your next letter.

I do understand your feelings of loss. Losing a childhood friend is like losing a part of one's life that no one else can replace. Nothing compensates for that hole in your life. Your story about a time with Danny is something you'll always keep close to your heart.

Having use of your boss's car will surely make a big difference to your daily schedule. You'll be able to interview many more people and your news items will concern places further afield from Numurkah.

Mention of Ben Lomond brings back memories for me too. Once, for our summer holidays (I was about eight years old), my parents took me on a holiday to Scotland. We stayed at a guesthouse at Fort

William. That's a town near to another 'Ben', Ben Nevis, which is the best-known Munro. Munros are Scottish mountains over three thousand feet. My father was a keen climber and his aim was to climb every Munro. I think there are over two hundred of them in the Highlands. The thing I remember about the holiday is Mum and me touring the town while Dad was climbing. I also remember the town of Glen Nevis, where we shopped for woolly hats and Highland toffee. Although it was summer, it was very cold. Thank you for reminding me about good times with my parents. I do miss them and wish they were with me now.

Australia is so very far away and our lives are at odds with each other but this makes our correspondence interesting and enlightening. I'm looking forward to your next letter,

Your friend,

Caitlin

22

Harry

Numurkah

30 May 1922

Dear Caitlin

It was great to get your last letter. I liked the bit about your parents. It's the first time I've heard you mention them and I realise now how difficult life has been for you. Although you were well cared for by your adopted family, as my mother would say, 'There's nothing like your ain folk.' I'm wondering if we ever stop grieving for our lost ones.

On a cheerier note, I've enclosed some snaps I took with my Brownie box camera. I've written the information on the back of each one. I wanted you to get an idea of where I live. About the 'high country': that's just a label put on a range of mountains in Victoria. They were named in 1836 after the Grampians in his native Scotland by Sir Thomas Mitchell, a Scottish explorer. So our letters have a strong Scottish connection and that will really please my mother – mind you, she doesn't get to read them but I will tell her about the mountains.

Next time, I'll tell you about the mouse plague. Or maybe I won't – don't want you to think that nasty things happen in Australia. I hope you and Joseph are happy in each other's company.

Cheers until next time,

Harry

23

Caitlin

Harry's photos showed his house with a picket fence at the front. What looked like a slate pathway led from the gate to a veranda that extended along the front before turning corners to right and left of the building. Fretwork trimmed the length of the tiled roof. Windows at each side of the door were barely visible through the branches of a giant tree in the front yard. He'd written, 'House front. Yarrawonga white gum' and 'newly painted paling'. Under the windows were pots of flowers of some kind. Without colours, it was difficult to identify them. Besides, they might be blooms I'd never heard of – that's a question for my next letter.

In another picture, Harry stood tall beside a woman almost half his size. He wrote, 'This is my mother, Lettie. See how tiny she is.' They were both smiling into the camera and I wondered who had worked the camera…next letter question. I could see that Lettie wore a dress with a white lacy collar.

Next was a snap of the backyard. He'd labelled each tree in tiny print: apricot, fig, orange and lemon. Apart from the fig and citrus trees, the branches of the others were bare and black. It must have been winter when the images were taken. That puzzled me, because I'd understood Australia was a land of perennial sunshine.

There was a photo of the shed where his motorbike sat proudly in the centre. Bonza the dog sat patiently in front as if waiting for a promised adventure.

A photo of Melville Street, the main street of the town, showed a sign. The names 'Pollock and Duthie General Grocers' were blazened above the entrance and a man in a white apron stood at the front door. I noticed another shop labelled 'Saddler'. Other images showed the post office and the river (I guessed that to be Harry's beloved Broken Creek).

A picture with a sign declaring 'Numurkah Primary School Est 1879' was presumably the school where Harry had his primary education. Groups of boys and girls filled the yard. The girls wore white pinnies and a man in a hat stood in a commanding posture facing the children.

A picture of a wooden church with a thatched roof was especially interesting because Patrick had told me he knew Harry to be agnostic and their points of difference were the basis for long debates.

24

Caitlin

Langley, Berks
29 June 1922

Dear Harry

Thank you for the photos and descriptions. Looking at them made me feel I was sharing time with you. I do enjoy reading about your life in Numurkah. Question 1: due to lack of colour, I couldn't identify the flowers in the pots. Let me know next letter. Question 2: who took the photos? Can your dog really operate a camera?

I must say your mother sounds like one of those happy souls who add pleasure and adventure to people who cross her path. Your earlier story about a trip to the snow intrigued me – such a journey. I'm guessing that you don't do that very often. My knowledge of Australia is sadly lacking, so today I'm off to our local library to search out books about it. I can't imagine what it would be like to celebrate Christmas in summer when the days are long and people wear light clothing and sun hats. That would be a drastic change for anyone used to our long grey winter days.

Molly and Michael are besotted with the their baby and with each other. Seeing them together emphasised my loneliness.

Now my home is quiet again but Mrs Blainey keeps an eye out for us and loves to spend time with Joseph. If the weather is too wild and I need to get to the local baker or butcher, she'll look after him for me. It's as if she's a substitute grandma and it gives her respite from her cares about Martin. Sometime soon, Joseph and I are taking a trip to Ireland to spend time with Kate and Bridie.

About my parents: they were victims in the Quintinshill rail disaster in May 1915. Over two hundred soldiers from a battalion of Royal Scots on their way to France, plus nine passengers, were killed. My father wanted to conquer Ben Hope, the most northerly Munro in the Scottish Highlands. The last time I saw my mother and father was at a time of farewell. Apart from social visits to Patrick's family, they never shared this space where I now live. When their faces appear in front of me, they're laughing. They're full of joy with a sense of adventure as they board a train taking them north. They're joking about getting remarried at Gretna Green – a famous destination for runaway couples.

Instead of an expected telegram about their safe arrival, I got news from an official of the Scottish Board of Trade that they were believed to be victims of this horrific event. Their bodies, and many others killed, were so badly burned they couldn't be identified. The remains of many casualties were buried in a mass grave near the site of the disaster. I daren't think of their deaths. If I did, I might hear their screams of pain; yelling for help that never came; calling and calling for help and no one hearing.

As I'd been staying at Kate's when my parents left, it was an easy decision to arrange my moving in permanently. The O'Hare family welcomed me as if I was another daughter and sister. I'd known Bridie, Molly and Patrick all my life and they became my siblings.

From that day, Kate became the only mother I'd know for all the days of my life. Kate said, 'Well now, m'dear, 'tis a sad life you'd have on your own in an empty house. You'll have a home here with us for as long as you need or want it.'

I do appreciate your letters, Harry. Give my regards to your mother. Keep well and happy.

Your friend,

Caitlin

25

Harry

Numurkah

31 July 1922

Dear Caitlin

Thank you for your last letter. First off; thank you for telling me more about your mother and father. A shocking story, and difficult for a young girl to deal with. It's lucky that you had the love and care of the O'Hare family to comfort and support you at that time. There's much I want to say to you but the words won't come. I can tell you the main tenets in my life: 1. Truth and loyalty are prime standards for living a good life. 2. Experiencing the violence and destruction in the war has made me appreciate the richness my world now provides and I aim to ask for all the good things it offers.

The flowers in the veranda pots are succulents that grow flowers only in winter. My ma likes to have flowers all the year round. Each spring, she plants dozens of red and white petunias that bloom all summer. You should come down here and see them for yourself.

Did you know that border collies are the smartest dogs on the planet? And Bonza is the smartest of his breed. Having said that, I have to admit that he hasn't yet learned to take photos but we are working on that. The grocery delivery boy took the pictures of Ma and me. He happened to arrive at a convenient time and was happy to help. That's the thing about Numurkah: the people are friendly and without bias. Ma says that when she first came here as a young lassie, she was worried

65

that she'd be shunned like she'd been in Melbourne, but there was no such bigotry. The people liked her from day one and nobody minded her funny accent. She gets annoyed when I refer to her Scottish pronunciations as funny. She says, 'I've tried tae sell it, but naebody'll take it.'

I hope all goes well for you in Ireland. I read the other day about the troubles and their fight for independence so I sure hope you and Joseph will be safe and have a great time with Kate and Bridie. Give them my regards.

That's all for now, Caitlin m'dear. Looking forward to your next letter. Consider yourself hugged warm and tight.

Your friend,

Harry

26

Caitlin

The energy of a two-and-a-half-year-old determined a plan to travel to Ireland in stages. We set off by train to Fishguard on the Welsh coast, where we stayed overnight. The journey was easier than I'd imagined due to the friendliness of other passengers and Joseph's need for a long nap. While awake, he charmed other passengers with smiles and clever attempts at reading from his favourite picture book.

A distinguished grey-haired gentleman asked me his name.

'Joseph,' I said.

The man smiled and said, 'With those blue eyes, he'll break many a heart.' Then he went on to tell me about his grandson. 'His name is Christopher, we call him Christo. He's two years old, about the size of your little boy.'

My son smiled at the man and clapped his hands with joy. Every one in the carriage smiled. It seemed to me that this child of mine had the power to make the world a happier place by his presence, just like his father.

When we reached our destination, Joseph waved at everyone and called out, 'Bye, bye,' and beamed at each of the travellers as they moved into their separate worlds.

We made our way by cab to a guesthouse a few miles out from the town. Molly had recommended Partridge House, as it would allow Joseph space to divest some of his energy before boarding the ferry.

The architecture of the house was mock Jacobean style – two storeys with a mezzanine floor that at one time had been a musicians' gallery. I saw small-framed windows edged with black lead and inserts of coloured glass here and there. It was built on many acres of farmland.

Mrs Davies, the landlady, greeted us at the door. She herded us into a living room three times the size of anything I'd seen before. A fireplace took up one wall; a calf on a spit would fit easily across it. I was so very tired I could only eat a few spoonfuls of the supper of bread and beef broth Mrs Davies had prepared. Joseph ate none of it. He was a dead weight as we mounted the stairs to our room.

Early next morning, Mrs Davies's son, Hugh, rapped on our door. When I opened it, he was almost dancing – shifting from one foot to the other, his face red and his eyes bulging with excitement. He gasped loudly as if we were in the next room, 'Would you like to see twin calves being born? Better hurry else you'll miss it. Hap yourselves up tight now. It's unseasonably nippy out there.' All this came out in one breath and the words skipping up and down the Welsh tonal register.

We quickly threw on coats and scarves and hats and followed Hugh through the kitchen, across the house garden and up over a small rise. Joseph gaped at the back end of the mother cow. A mass of glistening flesh lay beside her and a shiny shape of red/black flesh was slipping out from her to lie beside the first bloody bulk. The mother cow turned her head to look at her young, and very gently began to lick the heads and legs, then over their entire bodies. Her movements were slow and deliberate.

Hugh stroked her and patted her with the tenderness of a loving parent. 'There now, Annie *cariad,* you've done a marvellous job. There now.' Then he turned to Joseph and me. 'Now you get to choose a name for these newborns. All our new calves have names beginning with A.'

Joseph had been holding tight to my hand.

I asked him, 'What name can we give them, Joseph?'

He stood astonished and dumbstruck at the scene before him.

'Do you like the name Aggie?'

He laughed and clapped his hands.

I whispered to Hugh. 'We'll call them both Aggie. Aggie 1 and Aggie 2.'

Hugh grinned approval.

We watched while the two newly born calves struggled to latch on to separate teats and, after a little while, strived to get up onto shaky thin legs with a nudge or two from their mother. Joseph giggled at the sight. His cheeks turned ruddy and his eyes glowed.

'Thank you, Hugh. That was something to remember. We must get going now. Ireland is waiting.'

'Don' wanna go,' my son pleaded.

'Can't stay, darling boy. Granny Kate is waiting.'

'Be sure now to come back this way again to see how they've grown,' Hugh announced.

I promised we would. As we made our way to the kitchen, Joseph kept looking back until he stumbled on a rock and nearly fell over. We reached the kitchen door. The smell of newly baked bread tickled our noses and loosened saliva in my parched mouth.

When we farewelled the Davies family and boarded the cab that would take us to the ferry dock, Hugh and his mother called out, *'Siwrne saff.'*

Joseph smiled and blew kisses, while I wondered at the universality of greetings. The words may be unfamiliar, but when wishing pilgrims a safe journey, the intention is locked in the voice and face of the speaker.

The three-and-a-half hour crossing to Rosslare tested my ability to tamp down the breakfast I'd eaten. The ferry roiled and rolled, behaving like a man in a drunken rage and pleasing only himself. It ploughed through the peaks and troughs like a warrior primed for battle. Joseph slept. While I watched over him, his face took on the same look of his sleeping father.

The vessel docked into a grey fuzz of fog.'

Joseph was grumpy. 'Cold, Mama,' he whispered and snuggled into the fur collar on my coat.

Struggling to carry him and two bags sapped my strength and coordination.

Then suddenly from the hubbub on the dockside, I heard, 'Caitlin! Caitlin!'

In that moment, Bridie's smile lit up the world. Joseph heard her voice and in an instant was on his waddling feet trying to reach her. She managed to find him amongst the baggage and bustle of disembarkation.

'Bridie, I'm very glad to see you.'

We stood in a long, warm embrace. She picked up my son and we moved through the crowd to a waiting car.

Once we were settled, Joseph showed Bridie his book about animals. He quoted the words attached to each illustration that he could say quite clearly. 'Ant el ope…bear…' He turned the page. 'Cow!' He got very excited and gesticulated and garbled excitedly.

Bridie understood he was telling her something important but he didn't yet have the words to make his story understood. I translated.

'Well now,' Bridie said, 'all the saints in heaven would be amazed dhat such a wee man could say all them big words. Now we'll head for home.'

'This is a big surprise, Bridie. I didn't know you had a car, and I didn't expect you to be driving it.'

'We were hoping you'd like this wee touch o' luxury, cos Maeve's cottage isn't what we had at Langley.'

'I'm sure it will be perfect. And especially if you and Kate are there – that's all that matters to me.'

We were so busy catching up on each other's news and enjoying my boy's excitement, I hardly noticed the countryside.

'Nearly there,' Bridie announced. 'Oh now, I forgot. Ma and Maeve had to go into town on business. A family they know is in a spot o' bother due to the father getting arrested. The country's splitting apart so it is. They were annoyed because they couldn't be here to meet you but it was an emergency. I have to pick them up. So, Caitlin, it's best that you and the wee darlin' go on to the house. I'll drop you off there. Eileeen will show you around. We'll be home before you can say a Hail Mary.'

27

Nina

William's impression of Nina superseded her lost sad expression. He saw a woman much like his German grandmother but younger. Nina's body was muscular with strong arms, legs and wide hips.

When he spoke, he looked straight into her eyes. 'I will read this to you in English: I'd like you to repeat what I say.'

Nina's face flushed. She turned her gaze to the floor. She seemed to shrink into the back of the chair.

William smiled. It was the smile of total understanding. He looked straight at her lidded eyes. 'Don't worry, it is only language.'

Nina blinked.

'The words may sound strange, but they are only sounds. So now, I want you to close your eyes and listen to my voice: Dear Mr Kenihan.'

Nina's head bent towards the sound. She clenched her fingers into fists.

'I will say it again – Dear Mr Kenihan.' He waited.

Nina's voice was hoarse as she stumbled through the phrase. 'Please accept my sincere gratitude…' Again, Nina struggled. '…for zending my son Karl's leave passes in ze tobacco tin.'

William waited.

Nina got halfway through the sentence.

William repeated it.

She reached the end.

For the next hour, student and teacher toiled at the short manuscript until at last Nina was able to read and speak the lines.

'It is consoling to know zhat Karl treasured these things. I am happy you arrived home safely. Best wishes for the future.'

William applauded her attempt then announced it was time for him to shut the library for the day.

Nina whispered a short, stilted 'thank you' to her young teacher.

'You are most welcome, Frau Grottenthaler. Would you like to learn more of the English language?'

Nina nodded and, for the first time in a very long while, she treated her face to a smile. She asked William if he would compose a letter to the Australian Harry asking him if he knew who sent the package with Karl's rosary.

'I will be here each Thursday afternoon at three o'clock. We will start with stories for interpretation then we'll look at grammar. How does that sound?' He pointed to the calendar on his desk and repeated, 'Three o'clock each Thursday, yes?'

Nina struggled into her coat. *'Ja, ja, gut, gut.'*

And so, each week, the young man and grieving mother colluded in learning and teaching the sophistry of the English language. The spelling and pronunciation of some words confused Nina. She was inclined to look at similar elements and give them similar sounds like 'dough' and 'rough'. William talked slowly through these challenges. At one lesson, Nina stood up, grabbed her coat and shouted loud German protestations about the silliness of this new voice.

'Nina, the endings are different from English and gender is not specified. In fact, there are three genders: male, female and neuter for things like tables and windows. You'll get used to it. I have faith in your ability.'

Nina glared at him. *'Einfaltigen Englisch!'* she announced and stomped out while still struggling into her coat.

The following week, Nina crept into the library, head down. She walked slowly like a recalcitrant child meeting an angry school principal. William pretended he hadn't heard her enter. He kept working on a list of duties.

Nina whispered, '*Es tut mir leid.*' Then, in a clear English voice, 'I am sorry.'

William smiled.

Nina brought a small dish from her bag. '*Das ist fur dich.*' She had used her meagre sugar, butter and flour rations to make a small cake dotted with sultanas. The top was shiny with a jam glaze she'd made a few seasons ago with blackberries from her garden.

William accepted the gift. He moved to a small one-ringed stove and put a pot of water on to boil. 'We will celebrate today with cake and tea and you will tell me, in English, what the ingredients are and the method you used. Thank you.'

Nina had written a list of the ingredients in German: *Feines Mehl. Zuckers. Brombeeren.*

'Now Nina, tell me in English.'

The session ended with laughter, and cake crumbs on the floor.

28

Caitlin

Maeve's cottage huddled inside a square wall of trees, and the valley it sat in was all that Patrick had said it would be. Quiet. Verdant. Green as ever a shade of green could be.

Breathing in the sweetest air, I stood staring in the garden. Flowers everywhere – riots of red and white and pink were all around me. The same colours Patrick and I had wrapped each other in before the war. Water splashed from a stream at the side of the building. Trees gave the light the appearance of an evening gloaming rather than mid-afternoon. The thatched roof of the cottage sloped almost to the edge of the green-painted door and small-paned windows sat neatly inside frames and sills of the same shade.

Eileen, a neighbour girl, met us at the door with a basket of fresh soda bread. While I arranged our bags in a corner, Joseph sat on a little three-legged stool. I noticed his eyes almost closing and caught him as he started to fall.

Eileen said, 'Maeve and t'others are annoyed at not being here to meet you – Kate had business to do. They'll be back shortly. You don't need to be doing anyting here at all. I'm ordered by Maeve to be lookin' after youse. And if it's not taking a liberty, might I ask how are you coping since your man died? Maeve only told me he'd gone. She spared me the details but I understand 'tis a hard road you're travelling now. I'm to make sure you have everting you need from the good God's provisions.'

When she stopped to take a breath, I asked her to show me where

I could put Joseph down for a sleep and where would I find the makings of a cup of tea.

'Sure now, dhat's no problem. Follow me.' She picked up our bags, one under each arm, and trundled along to a room at the back of the house.

A cot had been made ready. It held a pile of stuffed toys and the linen smelled clean and fresh as if the sun had kissed it. Facing the cot, a curved padded seat followed the line of a long window. A small brown stuffed bear sat in one corner, and in the other corner was a stack of children's storybooks.

While Eileen emptied our bags and stored our clothes in a chest of drawers, she chattered on about how much she enjoyed looking after Maeve and Kate. 'Bridie's a whiz in the kitchen so she is and now we've got a wean to cuddle. Does he like dhat?' Before I could answer, she changed the subject. 'An' what would you be likin' for your dinner? There's a nice big pot o' colcannon on the stove. Will dhat be suitin' youse?'

'That'll be just fine, Eileen.' I said as I laid my sleeping bundle in the cot.

Joseph didn't stir while I took his outdoor clothes and shoes off and tucked him in.

'It's just as well he's asleep, isn't it now? I mean, he'd be heartbroken to arrive tinkin' he'd see Kate and Bridie an' they're no' here.'

I whispered that Bridie had met the ferry but had stopped in the town to meet up with Kate and Maeve.

'Well, surely they mentioned dhat – must've slipped my mind.' Eileen shrugged and left me with my sleeping child.

When I was sure he was settled, I returned to the kitchen.

Eileen had started talking before I'd reached the kitchen door. 'While the wee boy's asleep, I'll show ye around if ye like. You'll love the garden and, oh my, what a blessin' it is to have the makin's o' a fine vegetable pie right at the back door.'

'First I need a cup of tea, Eileen. Show me where the tea things are.'

'Och, don't bother yersel'. Just have a sit down over here an' I'll get dhat. The kettle's on the boil.' She pointed to a comfortable-looking chair in a corner near the black iron stove.

Then she sat down on her hunkers, poking at the dying fire in the grate. 'I s'pose ye'll be wantin' a lie down yersel, so I'm makin' shure the fire stays alive for ye. D'ye see this black bit fornent the back wall now? Well, that's the damper and after ye bank up the fire wit' dross from that scuttle ower there…' She pointed with a brass-topped poker to a bucket by the side of the stove. '…ye pull the damper out and leave it so. That keeps the fire down and in the mornin' all dhat's needed is a wee poke wi' this.' She shook the poker at me. 'D'ye think ye can manage dhat?'

I had no time to answer.

'Och, it doesn't matter. The others'll be back by dinner time an' I'll pop in tonight to make sure you're all comfy, and again first thing in the mornin' so I will.' She left.

I gathered the silence about my head.

29

Nina

At her next visit, William asked Nina to tell him about her son. 'Try to speak in English, Nina.'

She started off well talking about Karl's work as a tour guide and ski instructor but soon lapsed into her native tongue. William understood and listened to her story.

'On one assignment, Karl got friendly with Horst, who introduced him to cigarettes. By the end of the tour, they'd puffed and smoked their way through a tin of tobacco. Karl didn't like the taste or the smell of burning tobacco but he liked to take the lid off the tin and sniff the weed. He never smoked again but he kept the tin and used it to store odd things like foreign stamps for his collection, sometimes an interesting pebble or leaf that he found on his wanderings and sometimes it might be a letter from Inge, his girlfriend. They would be folded very tight and small and protected from any prying eyes.

'Karl also played in the local brass band, which often performed at balls and special occasions for the social elite of the district. Strauss waltzes, polkas and occasional drifts into modern foxtrots were their specialty. On the night of his last Christmas before he left for the Western Front, Karl had played for local dignitaries. When farewelling him, Inge clung to him until the last possible moment. They were not sad: he would be home in a few months when the war was over.'

The Australian Harry Kenihan had returned the tobacco tin to Nina. It included two leave passes that had allowed Karl a short respite from the war.

'Thank you for sharing your story, Nina. Now, I have a little gift for you.' It was a small German–English dictionary.

Nina gave him one of her rare brilliant smiles and said a loud clear, 'Thank you, Villiam.'

30

Caitlin

A dancing river poured over rounded pebbles and edges of spiky grass. An old wooden bench under a plane tree faced the river. I watched its journey. Grey rocks barred the water and shoved it into eddies in corners to make homes for newts and tadpoles and an occasional frond of fern. The movement of light and shade on the surface and amongst the trees gave a feeling of being in a chequered forest.

It felt strange to be in a place where Patrick had played as a boy. I conjured images of him climbing trees or swinging over the river on a knotted rope. My hair stood on end. I shivered. The vision was interrupted by the faint sound of a car pulling up on the roadside. I listened. Doors opened and closed. Voices drew closer. Then three pairs of feet trotted along the gravel path.'

I moved to where I could see them. First came Bridie, carrying brown paper parcels. Two tiny aged women toddled along behind her, talking in Irish, each trying to out-speak the other. I thought, conversations in foreign languages often sound like the speakers are arguing. The topics being discussed in Irish became stunted and senseless when they reached my English ears.

I studied Kate's face and saw the joy of Ireland's voice written clear in her eyes. It seemed to me that the love of her homeland had softened the pain of her son's death. All three were oblivious to my scanning eyes until I stepped out from seclusion.

Kate said, 'Well now, Maeve, jist look at what the wind's blew in! Hello, me darlin', an' where's that young spalpeen I've not had the pleasure of seein' in the flesh for such a while? It's a bountiful wind right enough that would bring us such a treat.'

'He's asleep from exhaustion.'

Bridie: 'If you put the kettle on, Caitlin, I'll nip along and have a look at him before those two wake him up wi' their chattering.' She raised her eyebrows and jerked her head slyly towards Kate and Maeve who bustled along towards me. She winked at me in conspiracy.

In no time at all, we were sharing a pot of black tarry tea and thick slices of sourdough bread lathered with butter and bramble jam.

Bridie jumped. 'He's awake.' She scuttled along the hallway. Before Maeve and Kate managed to get to their feet, Bridie returned with Joseph holding tight to her hand. 'I couldn't lift him. He's so big and heavy now so he is. Isn't he just beautiful, Ma? Look at his hair and eyes – just like his daddy.'

Kate opened her arms. Joseph virtually jumped away from Bridie and burst onto Kate's lap. She hugged him then held him away from her. 'Let me look at ye now. It's been too long away from us you've been.'

His eyes sparkled. He stuttered tales about the train and the cows. He ran back to his room and returned with his book. Kate reached for it but he held on. 'It's mine. I can read.'

'In the name o' the wee man! I'm dumbfounert!' Kate said, stroking his hair. 'Did you hear that, Maeve? The darlin' boy can read! I never heard the likes o' that. He can read an' he's only two years old!'

Everyone laughed when Joseph contradicted her. 'I'm two and a half'.

Bridie asked, 'Joseph, how would you like a ride, on a real live pony?'

He answered, 'Yeth'.'

'Good, I'll arrange that – maybe tomorrow – but right now it's time for me to get our dinner on the go.'

Bridie searched cupboards for pots and cooking utensils. Then she gave the contents of Eileen's colcannon a stir.

Kate held Joseph on her knee. She whispered in his ear, 'Would you like a wee story while we wait for dinner?'

'Yeth pleath,' he lisped.

'Well, Joseph, long before English feet pressed Irish soil, there lived in this cottage a beautiful woman and her three handsome sons. The first o' these was Keiron, nicknamed Kettle because he played the kettle- drum that he'd shaped from a panel of an old metal door. The middle son, Timothy, was nicknamed Tumshie – he loved to eat turnips every day for his dinner.'

I listened to Kate's voice and watched my son's eyes shine with adoration. Kate caught my glance and winked. She waited as if she wasn't sure about the next part of the story.

'The youngest son, Gerard, didn't have a nickname. He complained and cried and demanded that his brothers give him a name. "Well now," said Keiron, "you have to earn it." "And how do I do that?" the wee boy asked. "Now that will take a special effort from you. Think about something you've always yearned to do."

'So young Gerard went off scratching his head and thinking, thinking about what he could achieve that was extraordinary. Something his brothers had never done. He thought about walking from here to the coast then ferry to London, but he was fearful of getting on a boat. He thought he'd stand on his head for a week but he'd get too hungry and his head would hurt.

'Then one night he dreamt that he stood on a tall mountain, just like the imposing Lugnaquilla that overshadowed this valley. People called to him. "Jump! Jump!" they challenged. He jumped and felt himself fly through the air and the wind whistled past his ears and his hair flew back. Suddenly, an eagle picked him up in its talons and sat him on a rock. And crowds cheered and clapped and called him Eagle- boy.

'Next morning, he told his brothers about jumping off the mountain and flying with an eagle. They laughed and teased him but in the end, because he'd told the story so well, they named him Eagle-boy and that's the name that stuck to him all the years of his life.'

Bridie and I moved out to the garden. In a far corner where an ancient oak tree had lived its long life, I noticed some kind of shrine. Bridie pulled me towards it. Smooth pale stones of quartz surrounded a statue of St Aloysius.

She whispered to me, 'The patron saint of students and youth.'

'Hmmm, appropriate.'

A wooden shelter, like a miniature church protected it from wind, rain and falling leaves and acorns. 'Patrick' had been carved into the lintel with what could have been a hot poker. An inscription read, 'Go easy to your place in heaven, Pat.'

Those were the very words Kate had whispered to Pat at his last dying moment. My heart jolted and tears coursed down my face, as if something had turned on a water tap behind my eyes. Sadness for the loss of Patrick balanced equally with the joy his son brought to this corner of Ireland.

And so, our Irish adventure shaped itself into lazily happy days. While Bridie, Kate and I swapped news about our separate lives, Joseph wallowed in their love and attention.

31

Harry

The first short note I got from Caitlin lifted my spirits and damped down the losses and horror of war. Each letter I write to her forges hope and friendship between us. I think of her constantly. Her face. Her smile. Her hair. Her kindness. I keep seein' her smile. What a smile. Now that she's alone wi' young Joe in that big house and the months go on, the idea that maybe we could make a good life here in Australia gets under my skin. It doesn't need to be in Numurkah, although this is a nice spot on the map – good fresh air for the little ankle-biter.

Maybe I should say that in my next letter. It wouldn't be right to be too pushy. I know she's very close to my dead friend's family. But they've moved on in their separate ways now. Yup! She'd be better off here wi' me.

'What ye reckon, eh Bonza? D'ya think there's a chance for me with Caitlin?'

The dog looked up at me. He tilted his head to the side and I swear he was laughing.

My mother appeared at the shed door. 'Ye talkin' tae yersel again Harry. Dae ye want an answer?'

'Didn't know you were listening, Ma.'

'Wasn't really. But I ken when ye've got some big issues on yer mind. Maybe ye should get out o' here for a while. Go find some pals tae talk ower what's botherin' ye.'

'I think I'll take a walk along the river and sit for a while. When's dinner?'

'Och, it'll be ready in an hour.'

The dog heard 'walk' and jumped to my side, tail wagging, eyes pleading. We set off, me dragging my heels, him frisking around like he thought he was a pup.

32

Caitlin

Next morning, before Joseph was awake, a neighbour arrived. He had a miniature horse trotting by his side. It wasn't much bigger than an Irish deerhound.

'Hello, I'm Kevin,' he said, holding out his hand when I answered the door. 'I believe this is a special day for some young person.'

Just then,, Bridie poked her head out the kitchen window. 'Well now, Kevin, you're fine and early. Be with ye shortly.' She disappeared for a few seconds before showing up at the front door. 'Will you be havin' a cup of tay with us, then?'

Kevin looked shyly at her. 'Well now, I don't mind if I do. I want to sit the child up on the pony so I'll hang around till he's ready for dhat.'

Bridie and he looked at each other. It was like they were each recognising something deep in the other. I wondered. Is there something going on here? A prism of possibilities for their future perhaps? I smiled at the prospect and said nothing.

Joseph loved the horse at first sight.

'Hey, Joseph, this is Duncan and he likes apples.' Kevin took a bright red apple from his pocket and gave it to Joseph, who giggled and held the treat to the animal's mouth.

When Duncan took it from him, Joseph jumped back with fright and refused to give the pony a second apple. When Kevin lifted Joseph up to sit him on the tiny saddle, my sweet-natured boy went into hysterics and all the bribery proffered to him could not induce him to cooperate. He was still sobbing in Bridie's arms when Kevin disappeared up the lane with the sad little animal by his side. Only a promise of a walk into Ballinaclush village for ice cream stopped the deluge of tears and brought a smile to Joseph's face.

One afternoon when Kate and I were having a quiet moment, I told her about my correspondence with Harry.

'Is it goin' to Australia ye'll be doin?' she asked.

'Don't know, Kate. He hasn't asked me. My main fear is that I won't fit into Harry's life or with his mother.'

She laughed. 'Seems to me, only a good woman could rear a good man like Harry and if he does ask, and ye want my consideration o' that, I'll say to you, follow your heart, Caitlin – ye can't do better than that. Besides, the babby needs a father and if I could choose, I'd put Harry at the top o' the list. We don't want you to be suppin' sorrow for the rest of your life, m'dear. We loved Harry and if he wasn't twelve thousand miles away, he could drag his coat through any town in Ireland. Caitlin, isn't it a happy home you want for yourself and our own wee rascal?'

'You're right, Kate. But I'm thinking it isn't a good idea to put too much into Harry's letters. Suppose he's grown bitter and angry. And there's you and Bridie and Molly to consider. You're all the family Joseph and I have.'

She looked at me keenly as if she was spearing into my heart. 'Now listen to me, Caitlin. If you move a thousand miles from us, you will still be as close as you are now. My boy is gone from us. You and his own darlin' boy are alive. So I think I'll light a candle for the propagation o' this friendship wi' the hope that it will foster a grand life for you. Knowin' that you'll be taken care of is all I need to know, so it is and ever will be. You know, Caitlin, I tink fate is slowly bringing you and Harry together with latent and powerful forces of love so it is. You have two roads open to you and wee Joseph. Choose where the love is, Caitlin, and may God go with you.'

Then she wanted to know the details about where Harry lived and what he did for a living. I enjoyed having a good long blether with her about things Harry had written. While Kate was speaking, Maeve fluttered between the sink, the table and the chair she'd risen from. It seemed to me some force held her back from interrupting Kate's blessing.

33

Nina

Nina Grottenthaler looked at her neglected garden. She rolled up her sleeves and donned her rubber boots, opened the garden shed and rummaged among the tools until she found her favourite Dutch hoe. The morning air was soft and clear and she stood for a minute looking at the clouds before starting to dig.

Her mind spoke in German but she forced the English equivalent out of her mouth. 'Out you come, you rotting cabbages. Out!'

While she worked, she composed a letter to Harry asking him if he'd send a photo of himself and some information about life in Australia and especially his hometown.

She talked to the soil. '*Lehr geehrter,* Herr Kenihan, Pleese forgif zis English. It would be kind if you would send me som news about your home. Also, I'd liken a foto of your place.'

She abandoned the struggle with language and decided she'd approach William for help, then concentrated with the garden. After an hour, she had salvaged two cabbages, some leeks, thyme, oregano and a small bowl of luscious blackberries. When she'd put the tools away and marched back to her small kitchen with her treasures, she raised her eyes to the sky and murmured a fervent '*Danke*' to the universe for the produce.

The next day after washing her hair and putting on the only summer dress and shoes she owned, she took a dish of meatless cabbage rolls and a small dish of berries to the library.

William smiled a welcome. 'Thank you, Nina. I've been thinking about you and wondering how your English was progressing. You look wonderful, like you've been in the sun.'

Nina smiled shyly and handed him the notepaper with her broken words. 'I want for your help with zis letter.'

Lehr geehrter Herr Kenihan
Nehmen Sie meine Aufrichtige Dankbarkeit für das Versenden mein Sohn Karl's Fotos und Rosenkranz. Es ist beruhigind, dass er bewahrte diese Dinge. Mein Land ist in Aufruhr und es gibt viele traurige Mütter wie mich, die sich fragen, wie dieser Krieg geschehen ist. Ich bin froh, dass Sie heil zu Hause ankam.
Die beste Wünsche für die Zukunft.
Nina Grottenthaler

It only took a few minutes for William to translate, while Nina slowly wrote her words in English.

Dear Mr Kenihan
Please accept my sincere gratitude for sending my son Karl's photos and rosary. It is comforting to know that he had treasured these things. My country is in turmoil and there are many sad mothers like me wondering how this war happened. I am glad you have arrived home safely to your mother.'
Best wishes for the future.
Nina Grottenthaler

'Now I show you my Karl.' Nina brought from her bag, the small tobacco tin that Harry had sent and the photos that Patrick had mailed to her. 'See how he shines. Zis is the tin I tell you about.'

The tin was labelled 'Players Navy Cut Tobacco'.

William studied the images and thought how, in another time and place, he and Karl could have been friends. He liked his face and the tall straight stance of his body. 'Does he look like his father, Nina?'

'*Ach* no! He looks like *mein Vader*. His *Vader* was short, fat, ugly man.' Her laughter hit the library walls and bounced back to her sad silence.

34

Caitlin

On a night near the end of our holiday, sometime between midnight and dawn, Kate died. Bridie was hysterical. Maeve was silent. Suddenly the house filled up with people. The local priest. A doctor. Friends from the nearby town. Church people. All came in various stages of shocked distress. Keening began. Candles were lit. Wailing and praying and singing time-honoured hymns punctuated by sighs and tears. Kate had told me stories about banshees and I felt that the archaic lamentations filling every corner of this little cottage were an affirmation of their existence.

Contradictory causes and reasons for this earth-shattering event were thrashed out, analysed, scrutinised and disputed. People talked over each other, interrupted each other, with no relevant reason established. The kettle was kept on the boil. Stew, chicken pies, great bowls of colcannon, cakes, scones and bread arrived and placed on available surfaces beside the essential plates and cutlery.

Joseph toddled into the kitchen clutching his favourite dog-eared book. He moved through the throng of people calling for 'Gamma'. Bridie looked at me and I looked at Bridie in consternation. How do you explain death to a little boy who is not yet three years old?

I took his hand. 'Let's go up to your room. We'll take your pyjamas off and get you dressed,' I whispered to him.

He yelled. 'I want Gamma! I want Gamma!'

'She isn't here, Joseph. Come with me for now.'

The gathering around us stopped their muted conversations and stared at us. Bridie turned away and stood at the kitchen sink pretending to fill the big black kettle but her shoulders were shaking and she had trouble positioning the kettle under the water tap.

I knelt by Joseph and held him close.

'I want Gamma,' he announced and looked around searching.

I picked him up and left the room. When we were alone, I told him that Gamma had gone away to a very far place.

He threw his precious book on the floor, stamped his feet and demanded, 'When will she come home?'

'Darling Joseph, she won't be coming home. You see, she got very sick during the night and she won't ever get better.'

He ran to the window and climbed onto the padded seat searching over the garden calling, 'Gamma, Gamma.'

I took him on my knee and sang the *ali bali bee* song. After a while, we joined the others in the packed kitchen.

Kate's body was placed in the front room of the cottage. Copper pennies covered her eyes. Candles were arranged around her. Mourners took turns to sit by her while saying the rosary. I stayed close to Joseph. Death was not new to me but his little life had been one filled with love and goodness. My own grief and shock were replaced for a time by concern about my little son. His confused innocence gave me the opportunity to hide away in the garden, where we sat until the chaos settled to tearful grief. I allowed him to pick some daisies that grew across a patch of grass and showed him how to make a daisy chain, but it was as if all the sadness of the congregation in the house had transferred to his pure sinless face.

People crowded into the parlour, where the sound of beads clicking got louder and louder as the day wore on to dusk. Low murmurs of the ancient prayer for the dead accompanied the click clack. 'Out of the depth I have cried to thee O Lord...'

Somehow, arrangements emerged for Kate's lying in and a requiem mass at the local church. News reached Molly and Michael at Oxford, quickly followed by their plans to reach Ireland. Murmurs of *De Profundis* continued through the night.

Each time I saw Maeve or passed her amidst the busyness of the day, her stony-faced expression reminded me of the face on a marble statue. When I attempted to speak with her, she brushed past me, saying nothing.

That evening, after I'd read Joseph to sleep, Bridie and I sat outside with a pot of tea between us. We had no words for each other. The shock. The decisions. The unbelievable finality of knowing that the lynch pin of our little family was gone, left us numb. When Maeve appeared, we shuffled along the bench to make space for her.

'No, I won't sit with youse,' she rasped, in a thick hoarse voice. 'This is all your doin', Caitlin. Telling Kate that you an' Joseph was desertin' her and us just killed her stone dead so it did.'

Bridie stood up, her head bent towards her right shoulder and her arms folded across her chest, as if she was protecting her sad heart. 'That is wrong, Maeve. An' wicked to say such a terrible ting.'

I looked from one distraught face to the other. At the same time, I noted Bridie's lapse into the Irish vernacular. Strange the things we think about at times of life-changing events.

Maeve glared at both of us in turn, her lips opening and closing as if she held still more words in her throat, but for some reason she let them fester in a lump of infected anger.

Bridie slumped back onto the bench. She sat on the edge sobbing and rocking and blotting tears that refused to stop pouring from her red, red eyes. I turned away from Maeve and holding my head stubbornly high, walked past her. When I reached the bedroom, I shared with Joseph, I put on my walking shoes and a warm jacket and marched out the door, through the garden gate towards the church down the road.

No tears came to soften my heart. I prayed for Kate. I prayed and prayed and prayed, hoping that my lost saints would show me the road to dealing with the pain that threatened to destroy my heart and soul completely. I thought about Maeve's outburst.

Bridie arrived. We sat silent with our arms around each other.

At one point Bridie whispered, 'Words can wait till mornin',
Caitlin.'

I nodded and tightened my arm around her.

35

Caitlin

For me, Kate's funeral passed in a daze. I don't remember any speeches, or images. My heart was like a lumpen ball of lead and no light touched my spirit. Maeve refused to spend any time with me or with Joseph. Her temper worsened over the next few days.

After the mourners had taken their leave back to their separate lives, I confronted her in the kitchen at breakfast time. 'I'd like to make peace with you, Maeve. I –'

'You'll never compensate me with sympathetic lies about how ye loved my sister. Just pack yer bag and leave. I never want to look upon yer face again. Another ting, your mob murdered fourteen of my people who were doin' nuthin' but watchin' a football match.'

'Maeve, Croke Park massacre has got nothing to do with Caitlin. Apologise this minute!' Molly yelled.

Bridie heard that and barged into the kitchen. I pursed my lips tight and signalled to her to do the same.

'Apologise to an English woman? Never in all my days will I do dhat!'

'Maeve,' I pleaded, 'Please sit beside me. I understand your grief. Please sit, just for a minute.'

She glowered a menacing look at me and stomped out. Suddenly, I remembered Kate quoting Yeats: 'to be choked with hate may well be of all evil…chief.' How could one who freely spread generosity of spirit be born from the same womb as one so insufferably full of antipathy?

Kate had counted herself out of the political labels of the time.

Nationalist, Republican, Loyalist or Unionist were issues she never wanted to be part of her life. I recalled her advising me against asking Maeve questions about Irish politics or anything about IRA extremism because 'She will bash your ears till they bleed and I'll not have you or the darlin' boy hearing none of it. You're here to see the best of the beauty of this place and I won't have your precious time with us besmirched by roguery or cynicism.'

Molly appeared and the three of us sat in silence. No words found their way to my mouth. My head spun in a kaleidoscope of words, sounds, faces, tears.

Molly whispered, 'Yeats said, "all is changed, changed utterly". My heart aches for you, Caitlin. I know Maeve has lost her sister and she's grieving but there's no justification for her treatment of you and Joseph.'

I had nothing to say.

Next thing I knew, Joseph, Molly and I were standing on the path, bags at our feet, waiting for Bridie to take us to her friend Kevin's place, where we stayed for the next few days. Molly and Bridie came each day to spend time with Joseph and me. That beautiful little cottage beside the river and scented with summer growth of colour had become a place of pain and horror and darkness. Kate's death left an empty hole in my heart, and Maeve's vicious outburst offended the very core of my being. I knew then that my future lay elsewhere.

Bridie and Molly accompanied us to the ferry that would take us to the start of a new, different life.

36

Harry

Numurkah

29 August 1922

Dear Caitlin

I'm hoping everything is all right with you and young Joseph. It's been a while since I've heard from you.

Yesterday, in our town, an event was held to honour the Numurkah men who fought and died in the war. A temporary memorial statue depicting an armed soldier at rest was set on a plinth in the middle of the main street. At the foot of the statue, people hung floral tributes, including wreaths made of laurel or rosemary. A proper memorial is being discussed but it will take a while before we see it. I saw Mrs Coffey in the crowd and moved to stand beside her. When she turned around, she tried hard to give me a smile. Some people exchanged stories. Some stood silently weeping. I saw representatives from the Red Cross and the Centre for Soldiers' Wives and Mothers. Veterans huddled together like a bastion of support for each other. The local brass band played 'God Save the King'.

The whole shebang depressed me and I made my way to the Commercial Hotel. It's funny, you know, Caitlin, watching the men in the pub doing their darndest to avoid talking about the war as if it never happened. A group of four damaged men sitting at a corner table mumbling among themselves were ignored by the boys at the bar. I find that really strange. I stopped by their table on the way out but none of them looked up to acknowledge me. I'm wondering what you would make of it all.

I walked to the river and sat there for a while watching and listening to the sway of branches and the sound of sliding water.

Please write soon.

Harry.

37

Caitlin

Langley, Berks
15 September 1922

Dear Harry

I apologise for this belated answer to your last letter. It sounds to me like you've had a bleak reminder of the carnage of the war.

My thoughts: when I see a young man's face that holds glazed staring eyes, I search for his story in his expression and I wonder who cares for him. A mother? Sister? Wife? The thing is, Harry, these faces are almost infinite in number – that is my perception.

I'm sure that you have similar thoughts. But I remember your kindness to Pat in the face of his disfigurement. You didn't turn away from his damaged features. The young men in the pub that you mentioned were perhaps jolted back to their individual suffering by the remembrance ceremony. Later, in the quiet of their own space, they'll be grateful that they've survived and in time will shape their world into a place where they'll be accepted for the heroes they are. So take courage, my faraway friend, please know that you are in our thoughts. Thank you for all your news. I especially enjoy the bits about your mother. Apologies for not mentioning that in earlier letters. I would love to meet her some time. She seems to be a true go-getter.

Harry, I think you'd love Maeve's cottage. It sits in the beautiful Vale of Avoca and is bordered by a stand of tall pine trees. It takes an hour to drive from Dublin and it's walking distance to Ballinaclush village. We walked there a few times to get Joseph ice cream. A large vegetable patch and a cultured rose garden thrive beside the Avonberg River that flows fast and deep a few yards from the garden's edge. My son had to be watched every single minute. For the first while, Joseph and I had a lovely time, until our world fell apart…again. Kate died in her sleep. It's too difficult for me to write about it yet. Perhaps in my next letter.

Joseph and I arrived home to a note from old Mr Wilson. He has invited us to pick apples from his abundant trees. We will gnash and slurp our way through more than a few while we pick and pack the fruit for the local market.

So cheerio for now. Write again soon. I promise to write more often. I enjoy your letters.

Your friend,

Caitlin

38

Harry

One day while walking with Bonza, I tried to figure out how old he was. I remember the day my pal Danny got him from a litter born at Ryan's farm. I remember we'd just had cake and ice cream for his sixteenth birthday (or was it his seventeenth?). All I know is that before we went to war, Danny and Bonza had been inseparable. It suddenly became urgent that I know the dog's age. Instead of going straight to the river, I turned onto Quinn Street. I saw Mrs Coffey walking home and called out to her. She was burdened down with shopping bags.

'Hello, Harry. How are you?'

'G'day, Mrs Coffey. How's yourself goin'? Let me take some o' that load off you.'

'Thanks, Harry. Would you like a cool drink or a cup o' tea?'

'I'll come in for a minute. I want to ask you something.'

Bonza and I waited in her kitchen until she'd put away tins of Foster and Clark custard powder, cakes of Lifebuoy soap, packets of flour and a miscellany of baking products. Then she put the kettle on.

'What was it you wanted to know? she asked.

'I'm tryin' to remember when Danny got Bonza. I'm thinking it was around the time of his sixteenth birthday.'

She looked at me and smiled. 'It's lovely to know that you think about Danny. Sometimes I think the world has forgotten him and that I'm the only person who misses him.'

'Oh no, Mrs Coffey, don't ever think that. There's never a day goes by that I don't think about him an' my ma is always talkin' about the high jinks he and I got up to. Remember the billycart expeditions when we thought we'd be millionaires? An' the swing across the river that got us into strife when Lizzie lost her grip on the rope and got covered in mud?'

'I remember that fine, Harry. Not only was she covered in mud: her dress got singed along the edges when you two scallywags tried to dry her off. She smelt like she'd been at the centre o' a cloud o' thick smoke.'

Mrs Coffey reached to a high shelf for a biscuit tin. She turned to say something to me. The tin slipped out of her hands and crashed to the floor. Some of the contents scattered at her feet. I bent low to help her pick them up and noticed tears sliding from the corners of her eyes.

'Here, Mrs Coffey, sit down here, I'll clean this up.'

'Oh no, Harry, it's fine. These days, I'm just too clumsy.'

With that, she turned away from me. I could see her knuckles whiten as she grasped the edge of the sink and leant her body against it.

The kettle whistled. My mind was in a tangle of thoughts an' I'd no idea what to say to her. I picked two mugs from a cupboard and made a pot of tea while she pulled herself together.

'Don't you be concerned about me, Harry. It's just that some days are harder than others and now talking about Elizabeth and Danny and the dog brings back the heartache of missing them.'

'Maybe it's no' such a good idea havin' me pop in like this.'

She reached out to pat me on the arm. 'Not at all, Harry. I'm always pleased to see you. Please don't let this put you off. Like I said, I really enjoy talking about Danny and I'm so pleased that one of you made it back. As for my Elizabeth, she was meant to be my best pal. But you know, Harry, I knew the pleasure of having my children for the years they were beside me. Those years were all good and I'm grateful to have lived them. So now, Harry, I say to you that you need to live your life for my two that's gone. Am I makin' sense?'

I looked at the floor and whispered, 'I'll do my best, Mrs Coffey. I understand.'

'That's grand. Now let's get back to where we were a few minutes ago.'

We chatted over our tea and biscuits. I learned that it was Lizzie's sixteenth birthday when Danny got Bonza. It was the second last birthday Lizzie had before dying of consumption.

I left Mrs Coffey and wandered home thinking about the last thing she said to me. 'You're alive, Harry. Make the most of it. If for no other reason, it will honour the boys that didn't come home.'

'Okay then,' I said to Bonza toddling beside me. 'I'll write to Caitlin, ask her the big question.'

The dog ignored the enormity of what was meant in that statement.

The next day's mail brought me the disturbing news about Kate and I made a letter to Caitlin top priority.

39

Harry

Numurkah

8 October 1922

Dear Caitlin

I was very sorry to read your news about Kate. You and she had a very special bond and it's hardly enough to say, 'Be thankful you had those times.'

I've been thinking about you. A lot. I'm thinking it would be just great to see you again. I've considered coming to England for a while but each time I get close to making travel arrangements, I remember what the English weather is like. The first summer after I came home from the war, I got badly sunburned and was hospitalised for over a week. The scars still show in places. I'm not complaining.

What I want to say, Caitlin, is that these visible scars are much more bearable than the wounds I revisit when I remember my time in France and the image of your Paddy's damaged face. The vision sticks to me like wet paper on skin.

I enjoy your letters, especially the bits about young Joseph.

It's a hot one today – over a century, so I'll make this short before this flimsy airmail paper wilts like wet blotting paper. The thing is, Caitlin, I can't say all I want to say in a letter. But we've been writing now since 1919 and I feel that we know each other well enough to have a chance of making a good life together in Australia.

Not that there's anything wrong with where you are, but now that it's just you and wee Joe, you're free to make choices that won't affect anyone else. People might say we're strangers to each other. They might see all sorts of obstacles in our way but I know that we like each other enough to hope this feeling will grow. Is this a proposal of wedded bliss? Too right it is! So what do you think, Caitlin?

Write soon. I'm waiting.

Yours,

    Harry

40

Harry

Numurkah

Still October 1922

My dear Caitlin

How stupid of me. If you do decide in my favour, you should know something about where you'd live. First, the shape of our house: rectangular. One storey. Built entirely of stone a foot thick. Four big bedrooms, polished wooden floors. The kitchen has a pulley where we hang utensils and pots and pans. A massive black coal-fired stove, where we do all the cooking, takes up almost a whole wall. A scarred and chipped mahogany table that has secret drawers under the edges takes up the middle of the floor. (Joseph will have fun with those, I think.)

Queensland box and English oak trees shade the windows in every room. From the back rooms, you can look out at fruit trees – right now there are signs of fat black Victoria plums and golden apricots, and the figs from our tree are the biggest in town. Each February, vines laden with sweet juicy sultana grapes hide the corrugated-iron fence at the furthest end of our garden.

In front of this there is a plot of the healthiest vegetables this side of the equator. We grow carrots, pumpkins, tomatoes, lettuce and cucumber. Are you salivating? The garden is divided by paving stones sunk well into the earth by years of tramping feet. I think it's better if I draw you a diagram. The leaves enclosed are from my favourite tree –

the lemon gum outside my (our) bedroom window. I hope you like the scent of it.

I'm sure my mother would love it if we stayed in her house but this is only a suggestion and will be your decision. I haven't mentioned any of this to her. Two streets away from our house there's a vacant cottage and we could rent that for a while if you prefer. The walls and floor need some attention but I can have that done in a jiffy if you choose that option. At the risk of sounding like an eighteen-year-old romantic, I'm mad with excitement at the thought of seeing you here in my life.

Write soon. Still waiting.

Yours,

    Harry

41

Caitlin

Langley, Berks

10 November 1922

Dear Harry

Thank you for your last two letters. The second one arrived a day after the first. My head is reeling with questions about your attractive proposal. I feel very close to you through our letters. I enjoy them immensely and do thank you for your friendship. I need to know more about what coming to Australia entails for Joseph and me. My main concern is our personal life. Where would we live? What about your education system? Hospitals and doctors? My brain is besieged by questions. Our local library will have general information about Australia's climate and geography but, if I do accept, I need to know what should I bring in the way of furnishings and clothes? How will I get there? When will I get there?

I feel overwhelmed with decisions but, like you said, since Kate died, and with Bridie and Molly building their own lives here, there's nothing to stop me doing the same. I feel excited about seeing you again but can't say yes until I know more details. In my ignorance, I may be aiming for more than can be granted.

More questions: would your mother and your friends find me agreeable? Will I fit into your social life?

Please hurry with your next letter. The questions are piling up.

Yours,

Caitlin

42

Caitlin

On a cool November morning, I'm sitting on a park bench watching Joseph and a neighbour child at play. Equally balanced on a seesaw, their faces glow and reflect each other's smiles. Woollen wrappings – hats, scarves and gloves – have been discarded and now lie abandoned on the ground. A letter burns in my pocket and I'm sure that smoke will soon pour from the Australian stamps.

Flowerbeds and lawn borders show dried, stringy evidence of last summer's abundance. A breeze blows from the north. Now and again, weak shards of sunlight break through to challenge stubborn grey clouds.

I'm amazed at how much my boy looks and behaves like his father. While constructing boats and cars and makeshift houses from sheets and chairs at home, he sings. His hair always looks wind-blown. Attempts to tame the dark unruly curls with brush and brilliantine are futile.

My attention had been fully focused on my little son – answering his incessant questions: 'Why is the sky blue? What makes birds fly? Why don't they talk like me?'

'Because,' I told him, 'they talk like birds… It's time to go home.'

He ignored me. I called again and tagged on a promise of pancakes. He raced to my side, and with a breathless 'thank you' we marched hand in hand to the park gate.

I felt in my pocket for the letter. Again.

Near the exit, a youngish man sat in a wheelchair. He looked like a bundle of blankets with a pale pinched face stuck on top like an afterthought. I was grateful for the wide brim on my hat that almost hid the anguish I felt. A woman in a nurse's cape and cap was adjusting a rug around the place where his legs should have been. As we passed them, I heard a quiet 'Good morning' and wasn't sure which one of them had said it.

Patrick's post-war face.

My son stared at the wheelchair.

I replied, 'Good morning to you,' and pulled him away.

Patrick's pre-war face.

The nurse smiled.

I felt in my pocket for the letter.

Later, when Mrs Blainey popped in for a chat, I asked her if she'd mind staying with Joseph while I went out for a little while.

'Och, yes, we'll have a game or two… Don't hurry back.'

Wrought-iron gates opened to paths that followed the four compass points. Dry-stone dykes behind a stand of tall yew trees bordered the wilderness beyond the church where the river flowed to the sea. I knelt down by the headstone showing Pat's name. I took the letter from my pocket. In a voice that matched the softness of the air around me, I read it to him. 'What do you think of that, Pat?' Only the trees whispered.

Suddenly, my mother's face jumped to the front of my mind. She was smiling and healthy and beautiful. I wondered what she would say about all this. I knew that the bodies of my parents lay somewhere else, but it helped to have a marble marker in their memory. The O'Hare family had organised it. It now rested near where Pat was buried. I wandered along to where it lay and sat on a nearby bench. I wanted to tell them that I had been well cared for by the O'Hare family. I wanted to tell them about Harry and Australia. I wanted to say so much but all I felt was a profound sadness that they would never know their beautiful grandson. They would never be able to help me with this decision. Then I remembered my parents' adventurous spirits and their easygoing lifestyle. When I closed my eyes and gave myself up to the silence of the cemetery, the thought came to me that the only person who could help me was me. Myself. This discovery was accompanied by a surge of strength pouring into my veins. I stood up, held my head high and walked homewards.

43

Caitlin

Harry's letter had been so long in transit that when I smelled the leaves he'd enclosed, the lemon scent was mixed with the tang of ink. Questions poured into and around my head. What about Bridie over the water? And Molly – I'd miss watching Isabella grow. I understood that their lives had taken on a different shape but they'd still miss Joseph and me, especially at Christmas time. Then there's Harry. Sometimes I fancy that I see him riding off on his motorbike, but the lines and curves of the landscape elude me. I thought about Kate's advice about our future and the lovely comments she'd made about Harry. And I thought too about Bridie's life in Ireland. A life of cultivating their garden and looking after the hens and pigs and gathering turf for heating with the constant help of Eileen. Bridie had written to me.

Dear Caitlin

I'm thinking of you, my dear, and thinking of the dilemma about leaving England for a future in the Antipodes. Caitlin, whatever you decide, I will sanction. And you know that if you become disillusioned with the Australian adventure, sure now, you can always turn around homewards. We'll be here. We will write long and regular letters, Caitlin. I know you have the backbone to do this. You have been on a long hard road and now I can see you, plain as the nose on your face, on a journey leading to light and hope. Have faith that your soul will be healed in a life of peace and love. Give our own wee darling a big hug for me.

God bless you, Joseph and Harry,
Bridie

It ended with a postscript saying that she was happily in love with Kevin, a pacifist, and she'd only come back to England to say goodbye to Joseph and me when she knew the details of our departure.

There was a time after Kate, Molly and Bridie had left when the house was still and quiet; my heart would heave with longing to hear laughter. For a long while, it seemed to me that all the sounds of nature had deserted me. The birds had stopped chirping and it felt like there had been an immovable lump of lead where my heart used to be. My spirit had been in a state of rigor mortis – too far gone to unlock the tears that weighed me down. Now, with a visit to my loved ones, I could hear the grasses waving in the breeze. Birds came alive. I stood in the back garden and laughed at the sun.

I read Harry's letter again. A possible future had flown through oceans, skies and cities to land in my hot hands. After lunch while Joseph slept, I sat cross-legged on the floor. Staring but not seeing the shelves of books or the open wardrobe door where Patrick's clothes hung. I picked at my hair and began to worry the coloured beads around my neck. Separate them. Back together. Separate. Together. As if I was saying the rosary.

I read Bridie's letter again and slowly, slowly, my mind cleared and I focused on what the words meant to me and to Joseph. My body relaxed. With her words of approval and encouragement, I felt comforted.

I looked out the window. The grey street was held at ransom to the grey mucky sky above. Grey houses fenced off with grey palings and topped with grey chimney tops. Black crows flapped their way to rain-soaked nests. Bare branches of winter trees reached to the sky as if seeking a blessing from some tree god. Kate's death and the outburst of venom from Maeve had weakened my spirit to the point of despair. Joseph needed a life where he'd be loved and nurtured. I realised that both of these things helped to make my decision about Harry, and the life he proposed, much easier. The way forward (or southward) was clear. I started sorting out my boy's clothes, and the story of my future took shape in the form of Harry and Joseph and me.

Next day, my time at the local library revealed that the population of Australia was just over five and a half million. The prime minister was Billy Hughes – funny name for a prime minister; I thought it sounded more like a farmer's name. I found a poem by Henry Lawson, who was famous in Australian literature, and when I got home to Joseph, we had lots of fun singing 'Woo-loo-moo-loo' to the sound of the radio news signal. He giggled his way around each syllable telling me, 'That'th a very funny word, Mummy.'

When I showed him the book *Nuttybub and Nittersing*, we repeated the title and laughed together. For the next hour while he played with his building blocks, Joseph repeated 'wooloomooloo'. Nittersing came out as 'nitthing'.

After putting him to bed, I pondered the thought, if I were to get up at this very moment and mail my response to Harry, what would happen next? Everything that joins my life to him speaks of love and contentment, but is this enough for a lifetime commitment in an alien country? Perhaps, though, I'd be amongst new friends, new life. Peace.

I tossed a coin. Heads we go, tails we stay. Heads came up. I bit my lip. Best out of three. Heads came up twice. I paced the floor. Looked around the room. Best out of five. Heads came up three times. Before I'd mailed my acceptance, another letter arrived, as if my thoughts had soared through the ether to him.

44

Nina

Bergenstrasse 42

Garmisch

Germany 3926

Dear Mr Kenihan

My teacher at library is Villiam. Villiam said I should write in English more to help me learn the language and to stop me thinking every second about my Karl.

Sorry to give you trouble, Mr Kenihan. I vant to know where in Australia the best fruit does grow. Villiam vants to see my trying writing English without his help.

I live in sorrow. The days where I watched flowers grow in my garden are far far away. My future is all lonely. All sad.

Would you answer for me the following.

What kind of work you do?

What size is your house?

How many children in your family?

What is the name of your mother?

I wish for your health and hope for some happy times in your life.

Frau Grottenthaler

45

Caitlin

I reread Harry's earlier letter with the photos and description of his house. I laughed as I scoured the four pages of artistic details. He'd drawn a stick figure that was supposed to be his mother and placed her beside a sewing machine with the name Singer visible on the shaded black body. Then he and I, arms linked, in the biggest bedroom. He'd drawn Meccano structures, balls, a cricket bat and stumps in the room he'd marked 'Joseph'. He'd decorated curtains with fern leaves and sat vases of flowers on little tables.

The letter was attached to a package that included photographs of the state school; Melville Street, the main street of the town; a small wooden church, Anglican; and a bundle of brochures about field days, the Mechanics Institute, and the Numurkah Caledonian Society. He wrote, 'To show that this town has a history of immigrants, and you won't be lonely.'

Like the opening of a vast coloured curtain across an empty stage, the horizon expanded in front of my eyes to encompass the other end of the world. I imagined taking Joseph to the school. Walking hand in hand past the houses and shops and people. What would the locals look like? Would they smile at me? Would they sometimes drop in for a cup of tea and a chat like Mrs Blainey does here? I dreamed and waited still and quiet for the sound of voices and faces of people and events that would colour my life but the only voices I heard were those of Patrick, Kate, Molly and Bridie.

For Harry, it seemed it was merely a case of packing a bag and leaving my life – the way you'd throw out an old worn dress. As if the clocks and calendars fled backwards, I stared into the past at the most wretched time of my life. The anchor that bound me to memories of my life with Patrick was almost immovable and England is the only country I know. There is a confusing interleaving of past and future. But this I do know: wherever I spend my life, I will make a home that is an island and fill it with all that is in my heart. Then I will know that I've done the best for my son. I wished I could absent myself from England and the Irish and feel myself in Australia. With that thought, gates of hope opened before me and I knew then that 'all shall be well. All manner of things shall be well.'

46

Caitlin

Langley, Berks
2 December 1922

Dear Harry

Your last letter was very much appreciated. I almost split my sides laughing at your descriptions. So much so that I have decided to accept your offer of a life with you.

My head is swirling with details about how to get everything done before departure date. That's right, it's almost all arranged. We sail in January and should arrive at the Port of Melbourne around the middle of February. Molly and Bridie are encouraging about this decision. They hold you in very high esteem and feel that this is a good thing for Joseph and for you and me.

I will write more as soon as I have sorted out the finer points. Must go. Got a long list of things to do. Now that I've made the decision, I am excited and looking forward to the future. The future…for the first time since Patrick died, I think there is a future for me. Perhaps it's time to turn my face forward rather than backwards.

My heart is thumping at the thought of seeing you again – and in civilian clothes too! I enjoyed the description of your house, and the cottage sounds like it would be a good option for us. But I don't want to offend your mother or decide until I see the place and meet your ma. I'm sure everything will turn out fine and I hope you understand my hesitancy.

My main concern is that Joseph will be happy and his adjustment to this new life will be short and successful. He has been practising saying things like 'too right' and 'she'll be apples'. He's been making up a little song about Wooloomooloo. One day I'm sure he'll have a fine tenor voice like his father. We have been looking at pictures of kangaroos and koalas to bring us closer to your country.

So, dear Harry, how would you feel if we live at your mother's place initially, then take a look at the cottage together and make a firm decision from that?

Most of our belongings are packed and the house is quiet. I'm waiting for Bridie to arrive. She will stay with us and accompany us to the ship. It's all happening, Harry, and I am nervous, excited, happy.

Yours,

Caitlin

47

Harry

During the years of his correspondence with Caitlin, when Harry came home from his job at the local paper the first thing he did was check for mail. Specifically mail with English postage stamps. If it was a lucky day, he'd call Bonza, jump on his motorbike and head to a quiet spot by Broken Creek. Today he put the latest letter from Caitlin in his pocket unopened.

Lettie sneaked a look at his face while scooping a ladle of soup into a bowl for his lunch. She held her lips tightly pursed while telling herself, say nothing, all in good time he'll tell me. Harry took a couple of spoonfuls of soup, then jumped from the table, grabbed Bonza and the next thing Lettie heard was his bike roaring into life.

An hour later, he returned whistling and grinning and glowing with happiness. 'Well, Ma, it looks like I've found me a woman.'

'Well now, maybe ye'll tell me who she is, where she is and what this all means to you.'

For the next hour, Harry told her about plans for his life in Australia with Caitlin.

'It'll be just grand to have a wee person running around the garden again. And another woman in the house shouldn't be any bother. If she is all you say she is, we'll get on just fine.'

'But Ma, Caitlin may choose to live in that rented cottage in Quinn Street.'

'That'll be fine tae, Harry. We'll sort all that oot in time. I'm sure you'll have a guid life wi' Caitlin wherever you hang your hat.'

Harry grinned and started a list of things to do around the house. 'First thing on Saturday, I'll get down to the hardware store and buy enough paint. These rooms will look good with brighter colours. I want everything to be hunky-dory for Caitlin's arrival.'

'I'll get started on new curtains for her room. How old did you say the wee boy is?'

'A few ticks o' the clock after they arrive, he'll be three years old.'

'So maybe we should have a look out in the shed for some o' the toys from your young life, eh Harry?'

'It's going to be a great life here, Ma. I just know you'll like each other.' He whistled his way through each room while jotting notes about colour and quantities for paint.

48

Caitlin

I left Joseph with Mrs Blainey and set off for another stint at the library. From the information I gathered, it appeared that the town of Numurkah was unknown to geographers. Details about Sydney and Melbourne were plentiful and I soaked myself in images of beaches and wide empty acres of bushland. I read until words began to blur and my head was in a tangle of doctrinal descriptions.

When I looked at the clock, I remembered Mrs Blainey and Joseph. They'd be thinking I'd got lost. With two more unopened volumes under my arms, I rushed from the building and made my way home in the dark afternoon through lashing rain.

The nature of emigration is that everything that has ever happened to a person, all fortune great or small, all events, the distance of thousands of miles, longings, bereavements, loving – all are reduced to packing cases. Within the next few days, carriers were due to pick up a room full of tea chests and cabin trunks. I hoped my mother's china would survive. The pieces of Waterford crystal Kate had given me were wrapped in layers of linen and placed in the centre of the biggest container. It was pleasing to know that when we reached Australia, the scents of my English life would be there to keep the love and the memories of good times around me.

While we waited, Joseph climbed on the crates asking, 'Where ith my red buth, Mummy? When will I thee it again? Is it in thith one? What's in thith box? When ith Bridie coming?' His questions were accompanied by jumping here and there amidst the detritus of our life.

I sighed with relief when he got too tired to chatter. I gave him a piece of bread spread with jam and a cup of cocoa to drink, then it was bedtime. A major drama began when he reached under his pillow for Milton and couldn't find him.

'He muth be in one of the boxtheth.'

'No, Joseph. He is here somewhere. Let's look under the bed.'

'No, Mummy. He'th not here.' Joseph thumped his pillow with two little clenched fists.

I ignored his temper and slid my hand along the edge of his quilt and felt two small hard buttons. 'Look, Joseph! Here he is!

He grabbed his beloved dog and smothered it against his chest. A few minutes into the story he'd selected and he was sound asleep. Smiling.

Boxes of Patrick's books sat neglected beside two swollen suitcases filled with family photos and tokens that held the story of O'Hare family history. A film of dust had settled over them since I'd started packing. I giggled at the notion that lives can be stored in boxes. The giggle grew into laughter. The laughter grew louder. I fell in a heap with a Niagara of tears gushing down my face. A nearby pillow gave me something to hold. I rocked back and forth and gasped for breath, almost choking with the effort. In that instant, a door to the only life I had known crashed shut.

The only organised corner in the room was Patrick's desk. The shelf above it held folders of notes labelled *Paradise Lost* and *Literature of the English Civil Wars*; plus two thick anthologies of English literature. Copies of poems by Donne and Herbert lay open as if waiting for the owner to materialise and start reading where they'd left off.

I staggered to my feet and speared my eyes into the mess hoping that somehow things would arrange themselves by some kind of magic; that all these possessions would somehow acquire the energy and motivation needed to transform chaos into order. But the problem with inanimate objects is that they're just there; defiant in their presence, ruling your time and space and sapping your energy. They don't encourage, participate or support. I sank down amongst the mess. Immobilised. When I eventually stood up, I lost my balance and stumbled against the desk.

I checked Joseph. He was still asleep, still clutching his beloved dog. I decided to lie down for a little while to breathe my worries away.

The next thing I knew was the sound of Bridie's voice. 'Caitlin, Caitlin, it's me, Bridie.'

'Oh Bridie, I'm so sorry. I must've slept.

'Och, well now, you must've needed a rest, Caitlin. I just got a bit worried about you and your trachles, I decided to surprise you. I'll put the kettle on and you can tell me what stage of the big move you're at.'

We sat opposite each other at the kitchen table.

I hugged my cup of hot tea and told Bridie about the dream I'd just had. 'I stood at the end of a long grey street in a misty rain and light fog. The street was lined on one side with grey houses. The walls on one house had ivy strangling the bricks up to the gables. It badly needed a trim. A big grey door had tarnished brass fittings.

'The other side of the road edged a park that had oak trees and green shrubs and wooden benches. The sun shone on a man sitting with his back to me. His features were indistinct and he was dressed for summer in white short-sleeved shirt and light-coloured trousers. He held a wine glass that rested on the arm of the bench. There was a pond with black swans and a little dinghy waltzing with the movement of the water.

'I tried to cross the road towards him. But the mud underfoot held me still. I felt confined to the spot where I stood. Then I was standing in front of a wall. A door in the middle of the wall had no handle or keyhole. It was the colour of ochre. I saw some footholds and started to climb. The river had changed its course from north to south. It sparkled in the sun and was full of fish and plants and all around it was prosperity. I turned my face to the sun and felt gratefully excited.'

Bridie slapped her hands to her cheeks. 'Well, Caitlin, I tink dhat's a premonition about your life in Australia. It is shurely going to be wonderful, and dhat's truly good to know so it is. The bit about the sun means that God and all the blessed saints are watching out for you, doesn't it now. So now we'll make a list of priorities. Where amongst all this mess will I find something to write on and a pencil?'

'Bridie, you are truly a godsend this day. You're just who I needed.'

Just then a small voice was heard from upstairs. 'Mummy, Mummy. Where are you?'

'Well now, the darlin' boy's callin', and it's happy I'll be to see him again. You enjoy your tea while I give him a surprise, eh?'

It was like a competition between Joseph and Bridie to see who could get words out the fastest. Joseph counted the stairs, and Bridie said he was cleverer than anyone she knew.

Between us, a list of matters labelled urgent or important transpired. What clothes to put in the cabin luggage. Light summer wear for reaching hot weather. Books to read. More precious china and glassware to be wrapped and packed. Favourite toys for Joseph. The box of photos of my parents and the story of the train crash where they'd died. Insect deterrent. Handbag contents: notebook, pen, tickets, money, bankbooks, face cream, hankies, small first-aid pack. All were lined up, checked and rechecked.

'There's a snell wind out there, Caitlin, the kind we get before it snows. Too cold to take Joseph to the park. That's what I was plannin' for this afternoon. So we'll just sit here around the fire and sing a song or two like we did in the ould days before disaster struck. Maeve is so full of sorrow, we never get a smile out o' her, never mind a song.

Bridie showed Joseph the actions for 'Twinkle Twinkle Little Star' and Joseph clapped his hands.

When she started to sing 'Ali Bali Bee', he jumped off her lap saying, 'Gamma song! Gamma song!'

Bridie choked and pushed her tears back. I started poking at the fire.

'Everting is going to be fine, Caitlin. Shurely now it's a good decision you've made.'

The rest of the day was spent ticking off items on the list.

49

Caitlin

While waiting for the carters to pick up our boxed life, I thought about Patrick and how he'd loved this place. I asked the walls, 'Who will know you've passed this way? That you once slept through the brush of wind from these sheltering trees and the tap tap tap of the chestnut tree against the window. Who in this land will know that you once climbed the wall surrounding Mr Wilson's orchard and stole some apples? When I leave this place, who will remember these things about you? You have left me lonely for all of my days. Do you remember how we said goodbye when you went off to war? Can you remember those quiet August Sundays under the shade of a chestnut tree where we ate forbidden fruit? The dearest dreams of mine are lonely with the need for you. I'm happy to think that you knew how much I loved you. If I could make a song for you, it would be about the sound of laughter and the sight of daffodils in an English garden.'

Dreaming

A dream lurches through my life
It fumbles sleep and daytime routines
It flounders and whimpers at meal times
and word-searching seconds.
I am weak with longing to capture it,
to remember features framed in a reverie of the past.
A smile, a dimpled chin, strong bold shoulders.
You were loving until other latitudes claimed you
and killed the dream still stumbling through my days.

Watching from the kitchen window, I noticed that the branches of the mulberry tree were almost touching the leaves that slowly composted around its roots. I thought about the jars of preserved berries lining the shelves of the back pantry.

A loud knock on the door announced the arrival of the transport agent. He was a tall man with a fat round belly. One of his shirt buttons had come undone and his open rain jacket was outside-in. He bustled around the kitchen sorting papers and moving chairs to give him maximum room. He took a wrinkled hankie from an inside pocket (now outside) and sopped the rain from his face, missing the drips that fell from his hair onto the papers he'd piled on the table. Two younger men arrived and the fat man gave orders.

'Get to work, you two. We don't have all day, you know.'

A wrinkled piece of packing canvas had wormed its way from its original flat position, making rivulets of sheeting to cause the youngest man to trip. His expletives were loud and long.

As I watched the progress of the men, my senses were invaded by the sounds of past conversations about events planned around the kitchen table. Somehow today, these seemed louder and more vibrant than when they'd happened. It was as if the walls had absorbed them and were doing a reprise through a megaphone. I remembered the faces of friends who'd shared times with me in this house and embraced the sounds of laughter.

For the next while, the men humphed crates, suitcases and cabin trunks down stairs, and a couple of boxes from the parlour. They checked the labels on each piece.

'You sure this big trunk is for the journey?' the fat man asked, with a look that implied that I had overpacked.

'Yes, I'm sure.' And glared at him. 'Please be careful.' I asked again, 'Where did you put the suitcase marked "Books"?'

He pointed with a stubby dirty finger.

'Make sure these are marked "FRAGILE". They need to be handled with care.'

One of the younger men shrugged a definite dismissal. 'We know that, missus.'

The fat man grunted, 'I know my job, missus. Don't you worry, If anything arrives in bits, it'll be somebody else's blame, no' mine.'

Bridie popped her head out from the kitchen at that point and glared at him. I put a finger to my lips signalling silence. She shrugged and went back to play pat a cake with Joseph.

Outside, I heard a pair of lace-necked doves cooing to each other as they trotted around picking up a crumb here, an insect there, oblivious to the changes happening around them. Now and again the song of a blackbird could be heard, accompanying the protective 'woofs' of the dog next door as it sensed passing footsteps.

A faint outline of where pictures or ornaments had adorned the walls showed their size and shape. As the curtains moved gently in the breeze from the open door, it was as if they waved a kindly farewell. They billowed now and again and spread to extend the space that allowed the sun through to lighten the room.

50

Caitlin

The house was quiet. Ghosts stalked the rooms. The clock ticked time away. I sat on the floor and felt past simple rhythms as they pulsed and beat around me. Impressions of faces superimposed on the walls and cupboards. Images of past times crowded out any thoughts of the direction I am about to venture on. I saw a jostling scene of Christmas Day. Table laden with colours of roast beef, glazed ham and shivering jellies. The scent of spices from fat fruity Christmas cake touched my nostrils. Half empty wine glasses. Walls hung with loops of coloured paper – orange, gold and white flames festooning the walls of the fireplace.

If this house was a book, it would be marked by thumbprints and marginalia. Coloured bits of wool or slivers of newsprint torn from the tops of the daily paper would mark special pages. Discreet little pencil dots would tell where special words appealed to the readers. It would show how a variety of readers had perused the pages just as the stack of cartons and crates tell the story of my life. And people would read stories of challenges confronted and victories achieved and friendships nurtured and some sad times that balanced the whole. It would be a noble work with phrases that jarred the conscience and inspired seren-dipitous research.

Apart from the practical household things like linen and clothing, I packed the dress I'd worn at my marriage to Patrick and two of his precious books – *Selected Poetry* by Yeats and *Dubliners* by James Joyce. Because I wanted to take something that would remind Joseph of his father, I wrapped Patrick's letters and journal notes in a soft cloth and put them in a box for him. When he's older, perhaps he'll want to read the words of love that had swaddled him before he was born. I took my wedding ring off. My hands shook as I placed it in the box. I forced to the back of my mind the memory of the day of my wedding to Patrick, and closed the lid.

Mrs Blainey came in to say goodbye. I gave her Kate's precious teapot and cruet set that had been the centrepiece of their many cups of tea. I hugged her tight. 'I do hope Martin improves and in time will find useful work to take his mind off the war and all that entails.'

Mrs Blainey's eyes filled. 'Caitlin, don't you worry about that. Things will be what they will and we will get through it together. I'd really like it if you'd write to me now and again, just to let me know that you're well and that life in Australia was worth the journey. I fairly miss Kate and all our blethers. Don't you be worrying about Maeve's treatment of you…she will get her own comeuppance.'

I watched as she walked down the path and turned the corner to her own house. Over breakfast next morning, while Joseph entertained himself trailing raindrops on the window with his index finger, in walked Molly.

'Couldn't let you go without a last goodbye, Caitlin.'

Bridie said, 'Goodness me, look what the wind blew in. Where's Isabella?'

'Well now, she's with Michael, I didn't want her to see us all weeping and wailing when these two beautiful people leave. Now, Caitlin, are you absolutely sure this is what you want? I mean, I heard Australia is riddled with snakes.'

'Now, Molly, haven't you heard that the man who owns a big estate called Vaucluse near Sydney had tons of Irish soil scattered over his property and snakes are unknown there. Numurkah's not far from there so I'm sure we're all protected. Even so, Bridie has just given me a bag of the precious dirt that I'll spread at the front door to Harry's house. So you see, Molly, we will be safe.'

That afternoon, we walked around Langley knowing it would be the last time we'd do it. Somehow, to me, the shops seemed less colourful, less attractive. Was this a sign that I'd already left? For a short time during that day, it felt like the three of us were young girls again and the entire world was before us. Now, two of us were mothers, the house that'd been our home was about to be occupied by strangers, and our separate futures would be lived in three different countries.

When I settled Joseph into bed that night, I asked if he'd had a good time.

'I liked chathing raindropth.' He smiled like an angel, closed his eyes and slept.

I wrote him a little ditty from a memory of his father When he and I were happy. It would be read to him in the morning.

Raindrops

Noses pressed against the window
Watching raindrops roll along
She sighs, he whistles softly
A short one-note song.

51

Harry

Every time I pulled my work jacket on, the rustle of paper from the inside pocket reminded me that somewhere in Germany a sad old woman was mourning the loss of her son. And I had an opportunity to shift her focus if only for a brief light moment. Especially when Caitlin arrives, she'd be getting every blessed second of my attention. That night after dinner when Ma was out, I wrote to Frau Grottenthaler.

*

47 Meiklejohn Street

Numurkah

Victoria

Australia

Dear Frau Grottenthaler

Thank you for your letter. Thank you also for taking an interest in my life in Australia. I hope you are enjoying the challenge of learning another language. I am honoured that you'd ask me for information.

My home town is near the fruit-growing centre of this part of our big country. Local orchards are glutted with apricots, pears, apples and every kind of citrus fruit that grows.

I live with my mother, Lettie, in an old house that has four big bedrooms and a large garden with fruit trees. My mother makes jams and preserves and shares the surplus produce with neighbours.

I have no siblings. I work in the local newspaper office and ride my motorbike most weekends.

I think it would be a good idea if you called me Harry. Australians are less formal than Europeans.

Feel free to write again if you have any more questions.

Good luck with your English skills.

Wishing you good health.

    Harry

52

Caitlin

Emotions at this farewell overwhelmed me. My heart pulsed with desperation, triumph, a secret burst of laughter; all coming from deep heart haunts. Tears came in torrents and I understood then that my connection to this place, these dear people, was forged from my soul and unbreakable. Kate, the beloved Gamma and my mentor from my teenage years came through near and clear. At the edge of my consciousness, faces crowded out the appurtenances of travel – documents, destination and baggage.

The appearance of each face represented something once familiar. A past for which I will yearn and remain uncomforted until time and a better life heal the soreness in my heart. In spite of this feeling, it was as if I was hooked on the catching end of a fishing line that stretched over seas and mountains and cities, and nothing could release me. I could no more prevent the thoughts charging through my mind than prevent the sea rising on the foreshores of the world. I remembered Kate's words of encouragement.

In my mind's eye, a door opened and standing there in fair tall glory was Harry. I knew then that, whatever challenges Joseph and I faced, there would be words of love around us like a soft wind minding our lives.

While eating eggs and toast the next morning, Molly announced that we'd be spending the day in London. 'Tried to get tickets for a show, but it was too short notice and the comedies were booked out. So I think it would be a good idea if we spend time being free and talk about where to go when we get on the train.'

Bridie piped up, 'I know, we could have lunch at the Ritz…never been there.'

'Perhaps the zoo would be good for Joseph.'

Bridie looked at me with eyebrows raised in a question.

I laughed at both of them. 'All I want is to spend time with both of you…doesn't matter what we do or where we go.'

Joseph stared into my eyes and said one word, 'Zoo.'

'It's settled then. We're off to the zoo.' That was Molly.

Outside, the sky was black and purple. Clouds looked like they were ready to dump their bulging load at any minute. All four of us wrapped up in coats, scarves, gloves and hats before setting off for the station. Joseph was wide awake and firing questions at all three of us. Would we see cows? And horses?

Joseph loved the monkeys, hated the lions, and slurped his way through a giant ice cream. Molly wanted to shop for clothes but Bridie and I were exhausted so we settled for lunch in the zoo restaurant as a finale to our day.

On the hour-long return journey to Langley, all three of my companions slept. My thoughts returned to Harry.

> Love
>
> When first we were friends
> I forgave you everything.
> In the end, there was nothing to forgive.
> Was this your perfection?
> Our compatibility?

Next morning, a last goodbye to this place and to Molly. The taxi that started us on the road pulled up at the garden gate. We bundled ourselves into the car. Our odyssey began.

53

Caitlin

Bridie travelled with us to Tilbury. Her hands constantly fluttered around Joseph. Beads of sweat dotted her top lip and her cheeks were the colour of ripe tomatoes. While making our way through the throngs of passengers, stacks of packing cases and dockworkers shouting instructions, she clung close to us, as if her clothes were gummed to ours. Sea smells were all around me: diesel, iodine and sweat from cargo-shifting tradesmen. It took me a minute or two to identify an antiseptic smell tickling my nose. Creosote. A memory from long ago when the roads on our street were being tarred.

A crew member picked up our cabin luggage and we clambered up the gangplank behind him. Joseph took my hand and I kept my eyes on our guide. Bridie held tight to the handrail while placing her feet carefully on the wooden spars. Squawking, squealing seagulls circled above the mayhem and occasionally dived to the dock for abandoned morsels of food.

Bridie mumbled to herself, 'Blessed mother o' God, grant me patience and energy…' Every few minutes she'd call out, 'You all right, Caitlin?'

'Fine, Bridie. How are you?'

'Well now, I'm doin' fine but my feet are stingin' like a barrowload of red-hot needles. Shure now they're longin' for those comfy slippers now snuggled by the fireplace back home.'

Joseph turned to watch her. 'C'mon, Bridie. Watch me!'

'Shure now, just as long as you're in my sight, that's all the help I need.'

He beamed with this acknowledgement and waited until she caught up with him, and took her hand. I hid my smile as we snaked through corridors to our assigned cabin.

As if he was yelling to a workmate, the crewman shouted, 'You're allowed ten minutes on board if you're not a passenger.'

I heard Bridie muttering behind me, 'He's a bit bossy, Caitlin, isn't he now? Doesn't he know this wee darlin' is his most precious cargo?'

I turned and smiled an apology to him. He winked at me in a gesture of understanding.

'We know that, Bridie, but Joseph is only one child among many.'

'Well now, Caitlin, 'tis not from where I'm seeing it. Shure now, look at him.'

Joseph did an about-face from important protector to fun-loving child. His eyes shining with glee, and busily jumping on the upper bunk. With each jump he shouted, 'Look, Mummy, look at the thea-gulth.'

I looked at the weariness stamped on Bridie's face. 'Sit down, Bridie. You look exhausted.'

'I'm sick with sorrow at your leaving.'

I put my arms around her. 'You know that Joseph and I love you and I know that, to you, he is your favourite person in the whole wide world. But you know, Bridie, it's been a bad time for all of us. I couldn't have managed to make this decision without your caring support.

'Och now, it's silly I'm being. Don't' fach yoursel, Caitlin, I know dis is the best ting for youse. I only hope you are shurely takin' away good memories and Maeve's chastising doesn't stay too long in your heart.'

'Well, Bridie, I can't deny that it hurt, but losing Kate the way we did was like having my heart bashed to bits. Maeve can live with her own mean self. She will pay the price one way or another.'

Bridie stood up and we took a look at the flat sea from the port-hole. Seagulls soared silently below a blue sky dotted with small white tufts of cirrus clouds. A loud rumble was coming from somewhere far below and a scent of clean fresh linen assured me of sleeping in comfort. A cupboard took up one corner of the cabin, and a notice of welcome instructions posted on the door outlined available activities for each day. Bridie helped me store our travelling luggage in a tallboy of four drawers while Joseph had fun opening and closing each drawer and door. He shoved his clothes in the two bottom drawers, and pulled them out again repeatedly.

Finally, it was time for Bridie to leave. 'Now, Caitlin, you know you go with my blessing and I'll be waiting for letters telling me all about your new life. It's missing you I'll be and this darlin' boy.' Tears the size of a sixpence sat in the corner of her eyes, waiting to spill down her face.

I had no words to say. It seemed my tongue couldn't find a way back to forming any kind of sounds. We hugged each other tight, with Joseph between us.

I watched her bustle along and down the gangway until she got lost in the crowd on the docks. Crew members were giving rolls of coloured streamers to passengers lined along the rail. Joseph stood on a stool. Everything seemed in slow motion. A deliberate lowering of the gangway, an even slower cast off, then a final siren blast and the RMS *Ormonde* slid away from the dock.

Just as it started moving, we spotted Bridie waving a bright green scarf and waving her arms like a semaphore signal. People on board went mad with cheering and throwing paper ribbons of farewell to the crowds below. I couldn't be sure but it looked like Bridie caught one of ours and held it until distance snapped our connection. Passengers shouted messages from the promenade deck to family and friends still waving on the dock. The strips of paper snapped to litter and hung down the steel plates of the ship's side like debris from yesterday's party.

54

Caitlin

Our world has shrunk. For the following weeks it will be the four walls of our cabin and the public rooms and decks of the ship. It is stifling in the cabin. There is no breeze. Perspiration is a problem and I wonder if this is how it will be in Australia. The sea swells are like little hills on the move, smooth and grey like the sky above. Formal activities listed each day include shuffleboard, deck quoits, archery, dancing and swimming competitions.

Dinner for young children is earlier than adult sittings but last night Joseph refused to leave my side and I arranged to have food sent to our cabin. This morning, I enrolled him at the playroom, where he has made friends. Now he barely wants to know me. When I was putting him to bed tonight, he chatted non-stop about the games he'd played and all about new friends Toby and Peter.

'Toby said hith Mummy and Daddy are going to Adelaide and hith daddy built thith ship and heeth going to build bigger oneth. Peter speakth like Bridie and has two thithterth that hit him and take away hith bookth. They tell him he'th a thithy. Mummy, what'th a thithy?'

As I write this version of his day's exploits, I can't help smiling. He is growing up fast and I wonder what the extent of his vocabulary will be by the time we reach Melbourne.'

I would not have believed that anything could creak like this ship does. A mixture of metal and wood grinding against each other and heaving itself over the waves is sometimes comforting but other times feels like it doesn't know which direction to take.

Before leaving England, I made up pictures to fill the empty spaces of my life, and Harry was central to these imaginings. When I try to look at our future, I see love tempered with longing for the folk who used to be my family. Bridie and Kevin, Molly and Michael, and mostly dear kind wise Kate.

In spite of Harry's letters, the reading, lectures and talking with other passengers on board, I realise I have no idea what this new life will bring to me.

One thing that tickles at my memory: I remember Harry keeping us amused with stories about Australia, but I can't remember the sound of his voice. I try to hear the native inflections in the written language of his letters but the smile, the sound, the light in his eyes, all are left to my imagination.

Joseph has turned out to be a much better sailor than his mother. The first few days of the voyage have challenged my travelling confidence. The smoky smuts from the funnels are getting in my hair and I think by the time the ship reaches Melbourne, I'll be a total physical wreck.

At dinner time, if the ship is rolling, boards called fiddles are raised all around the tables to keep the plates from skiting on to our laps or the floor. At the end of our meal, children were allowed to join the adults and Joseph brought two little model cars with him. While others at the table were finishing their wine, he used the fiddles as barriers on a miniature racing track. His gleeful laughter infected some passengers and soon Joseph with his racing cars was the centre of attention. The noise of wheels and metal being bashed against wood soon slowed down. He crawled onto my lap, holding one little car in each hand, and slept.

55

Nina

Garmisch
Southern Germany

Herr Kenihan

This letter is to tell you that I am started proceedings to come to Australia. My friend William at the library is helping me to complete the forms. He knows Australian people in Berlin. Life is difficult here now. Inflation 90%. My old neighbour has died and so I think I will be better in your country. I maybe have accommodation at a place Shepparton. Soon I will let you know more. I hope that we can meet and I get to know your mother.

Frau Grottenthaler

56

Harry

Numurkah

Dear Frau Grottenthaler

I hope you are well and continuing to increase your English language skills. Thank you for your letter with the news that you will soon be in Australia. Shepparton is not very far from Numurkah. It is right in the heart of a busy, productive fruit-growing area. The trees are laden with fat juicy produce and summer is singing in the fields.

I have big news to share with you. The widow of my English friend is on the high seas now on her way to Australia. Her name is Caitlin and she has a little boy named Joseph. We are to be married as soon as possible after she arrives. It will be my pleasure to meet you and to introduce you to my mother and Caitlin and Joseph. Perhaps you will teach him some German lullabies. Please let me know the date of your arrival and the name of your ship.

Have a safe journey
Harry Kenihan

57

Caitlin

Yesterday, I felt sick and went up on deck to escape the clammy cabin air. A crewman told me that the sickness was probably due to the groundswell from Somalia. I wonder where, in heaven's name, is Somalia? It was never part of my 'learning Australia' programme.

I thought I'd die in the small humid cabin we'd been allotted. Only the thought of leaving my baby an orphan gave me the steel to keep going. A woman at our breakfast table noticed the pale yellowness (or was it green?) of my face and recommended I visit the ship's doctor. She offered to look after Joseph while I did so.

I abandoned the pancakes, bacon and sausages and staggered around corners and along gangways to find the medical office. Metal bars mounted along the walls were a godsend in helping me keep my trudging feet going in the right direction. Just as I turned the final corner, I bumped into a giant of a man. He was bent double and holding on to a bar as if his life depended on it. He was the last person in a long line of passengers seeking help. I'd never seen faces tinged with green before but as I looked along the line-up, degrees of sea green from foreheads to chins confronted me. I was glad there were no mirrors nearby.

The ship's medical officer was obviously anticipating a rush on his services and busily doled out injections to all. I didn't feel a thing as the needle punched my upper arm, and I hurried off to find Joseph and his carer. The woman's name was Elsie Wilson. Elsie told me she was thirty-seven years old and had no children of her own. Although there was no Irish in her voice, the way she bent to Joseph's height and asked if he'd like to hear a story reminded me of Kate. When she'd taken him to the children's playroom, she watched while he built a castle with coloured blocks and made friends with other children. He was so busy discussing his coloured construction that he hardly noticed my arrival.

Elsie was full of advice for me. 'Now, Caitlin, I think you should get yourself back to your cabin and collapse on your bed. I'll look after Joseph. He is a happy little soul, isn't he? I'll check up on you around dinner time.'

My protests went unheeded. I don't remember my head hitting the pillow and it seemed a very short time later when I woke up feeling energised and hungry. I checked my watch and realised I'd slept most of the day. It didn't take long to splash water on my face. While combing my hair, there was a gentle tap on the cabin door. Elsie and Joseph had arrived. He was carrying a flat piece of cardboard with a pile of red and blue blocks arranged like a tower.

'Look, Mummy, I built you a cathel.'

'He wouldn't let it go and the girl said he could have it and take it back tomorrow. My, you look a lot better, Caitlin. The rest has brought colour back into your cheeks. See you at dinner.'

She hurried away before I could thank her properly. Joseph stood looking up to me and beaming with pride at his 'cathel'.

Elsie was about five feet two inches and for dinner that night she was dressed smartly in a floral sleeveless dress of crêpe de Chine. It had a round neckline and a drop waist, and reached her legs at mid-calf. She had the creamy, unlined complexion of someone who'd never spent much time in the sun. Her chestnut-brown hair was piled high on top of her head, every hair tucked carefully in place with Kirby grips. Her make-up and manicure were modest and faultless. I wondered how she maintained that standard of grooming. I found make-up and hairdressing challenging without the space and amenities of my old home.

When I said this to Elsie, her response was, 'Get yourself to the beauty parlour – you'll feel a lot better.'

Jack, Elsie's husband, was a good foot taller than she was and served as a colour contrast to her. He was dressed in shades of brown and fawn, stylishly conservative. Skinny and lean, he looked as if his body had been shaved to the bone. With an impassive face, he appeared unapproachable. His deep-set eyes were the colour of gunmetal and looked as hard. I saw pain and tragedy in them. His black eyebrows were highly arched and one was slightly tufted. His nose was straight and below it a thin dark moustache hung as if it was tired. His black hair, threaded with grey, was thick and wavy. His face seemed to be constantly full of shadows.

Elsie and Jack were going to settle in Melbourne, where Jack's sister lived. 'You know, Caitlin, Jack hasn't been the same since he came back from the war. We'll never have children and we're hoping that the Australian climate will be good for his health. What happened to Joseph's father?'

'He died before Joseph was born,' I whispered.

'Oh, that's terrible. And you're going out to Australia all on your own? That is so very brave.'

'Well, I won't be alone for long; I'm getting married to Pat's friend from the war. It took a while for me to make the decision but I'm confident it will be the best thing for us.'

'Where will you live? I mean, Australia's a big place.'

I told her a bit about Harry and his hometown. Of course, she'd never heard of Numurkah.

'Is it far from Melbourne?'

'Not sure, but I think it's a few hours by road.'

'It would be grand if we could keep in touch. I'd like to know how you're coping and all about your wedding plans.

At breakfast the next morning, she gave me a note with Jack's sister's address. 'Keep that safe now. I really would like to hear from you.'

I considered giving her Harry's address but decided to think longer about it.

She wore a light bright pastel colour dress. Loose style of long sleeves, reaching mid-calf and buttoned to the neck. Each day, her dress was the same style but a different colour.

I asked her, 'How many of those dresses do you have, Elsie? It seems to me you've captured the complete stock of your local department store.'

She laughed and answered. 'Well now, Caitlin, I make all my own clothes and when I get to Melbourne, I'm planning on starting my own business, so you mind and keep in touch with me and I'll make sure you'll always have something nice to wear.'

Like Elsie, most of the people on board are hungry for adventure in new careers, and happy to escape the foggy dark winters of Britain.

Each day, I hover by the door of the playroom to watch Joseph interact with the other children. The young girl in charge has a lovely smile and her intelligent attitude to the boys and girls in her care reassures me. I watch her ask each child their name and guide them to a place on the mat. Joseph is anxious to take part in challenging car races, and in the creation of wonderful creatures from paper.

For the first activity each morning, the children sit in a circle at the carer's feet while she reads them a story about farm animals or foreign countries, particularly Australia. Her young charges are asked to make noises of horses and cows and frogs. I watch Joseph settle in to the hilarity and sneak away for a brisk walk and a swim, then I find a corner with a cup of tea and a book.

After lunch, we go back to our cabin. Joseph sleeps for as long as it takes to replenish the energy he's spent during the morning's activities. I check the state of our clothing for laundry pick-up, write letters, read and scribble notes for journal items. The few books I brought are packed away in a crate with our belongings and I was thrilled to find treasures in the ship's library; I picked *Sister Carrie* by Dreiser and *A Room With a View* by Forster and lost myself in the pages of excellent writing.

In a dog-eared copy of Yeats's poetry, I spied '...and he had known at last some tenderness. Before earth took him to her stony care.'

The lines reminded me of the time when Patrick lay dying and I felt so very, very sad. I didn't read any more of Yeats. Perhaps I never will.

58

Caitlin

Near Suez

January 1923

Dear Harry

The ship will soon be in the Suez Canal and I hope to mail this letter to you. We have settled into a routine of eating, sleeping, walking and deck games. Shuffleboard and deck quoits are not my favourite pastimes. I think that's because I'm continually defeated by shipmates who insist I compete with them. I'm looking forward to seeing contrasting activities at Port Said. Joseph goes happily to the playroom each morning and is very interested in the stories the young woman carer reads to him. Today's conversation went like this.

Me: 'What did you learn today, Joseph?'

Joseph: 'Well, Printheth Irene lived in a huge cathel far, far away and she wath very unhappy. Mummy, when we go far away to Aus…, Aus…, will there be cathelth and strange people?'

Me: 'Well, darling, if there are castles, we'll find them. The people might be strangers to us but I'm sure once they get to know us, they will be kind and helpful.'

His tongue gets in a twist with some big words – like Australia – but we're working on that. Yesterday, a young Irish couple befriended us and I was very pleased to hear once again the voices of Ireland. Siobhan sounded just like Bridie.

When I heard her say to Joseph, 'And where is it you'll be goin', me darlin?' I found immediate comfort in her presence.

Joseph stared at her for a long time as if he recognised the voice but understood it to be from an unfamiliar face. Her husband, Sean, organised a match with Elsie, Jack and me to make two teams for shuffleboard. We made enough fun to help the day pass with laughter and friendly rivalry. I liked Siobhan immediately, and forgave her each time she slaughtered me at deck quoits.

Sean taught me some Australian words – cobber, drongo, bludge, dunny – and we laughed at the sounds and meanings.

I hope all's well with you, Harry, and I'm longing for the day when we meet at last.

The dinner gong has just sounded, so must end here.

Love from Caitlin

*

Somewhere on the High Seas
January 1923

Dear Bridie

Somehow, I can't picture you in a place other than Maeve's cottage in Rathdrum. When I saw you there in the days before disaster struck, you shone as though the sun itself had found its place in your heart and mind. I can see you plain as I'm seeing the cabin desk I'm sitting at now. Thank you again for all your kindnesses to me and to Joseph. Having you in our lives is a great source of comfort. The distance that now separates us can't take you out of our hearts.

I do hope that you and Kevin can pull enough pleasure out of life and that Maeve is not being too difficult. I understand that times are changing the face of Ireland and many families are suffering. Please keep safe during these tumultuous times.

Joseph and I are having a lovely time. We have made friends with a young Irish couple from Dublin, and Joseph is the centre of their attention.

It would be great to hear from you, Bridie, and to know that all is well with you. To find a letter from you when we arrive at Harry's house would be lovely. Look after yourself and give our regards to Eileen.

Love and hugs from the high seas,
Caitlin and Joseph

59

Caitlin

We reached Port Said and mixed with other passengers leaning over the vessel's railings to watch a number of little boats approaching from the shoreline. Each boat was steered by a tiny dark-skinned man, while a second man shouted up to the passengers. They had baskets of picture postcards showing the pyramids, decorative fans for use on hot nights, tiny brass models of camels and pyramids, and one boat offered bales of Egyptian cotton. Elsie and I shared the cost of three coloured lots of it.

I bought two large pomegranates – a new taste experience. If I'd known that seeding them entailed blood-red stains on each arm and the front of my lovely white cotton dress, I might have given them a miss.

Some people threw coins into the water and the young natives dived to retrieve them. Emigrants lining the rail of the ship applauded and the merchants yelled to the travellers, asking for more coins. The scene took on a surreal circus atmosphere.

One morning while Joseph was in the playroom, I sat on a deckchair reading. The ship was scarcely rolling. The sky was empty of birdlife and the smell of the sea soothed my soul. I realised the light had changed. It was much brighter than the dull light we'd had for days. The glitter hurt my eyes. Some miles ahead, I could see the blue I'd heard the captain talk about. Suddenly there was a great commotion on the water. Creatures like giant fish jumped high in the air and dived back into the sea. Elsie and Jack came up behind me.

'Dolphins,' Jack whispered. 'Let's go to the ship's bow and watch them leaping in front of it.'

The dolphins were waiting for us just where the sunlight began.

Jack said, 'They like being watched by people on ships.'

I watched these beautiful creatures jump back and forth, moving much faster than the boat as if their energy source was much more efficient than the huge engines that powered the vessel.

As the ship moved closer to the equator, notices were delivered to cabins about entertainment plans for the crossing the line ceremony. I tried to explain to Joseph that the line dividing the earth into the northern and southern hemisphere was invisible. My words didn't make the least impression on his young mind.

The evening of the crossing was called Wog Day. Chaos erupted as first-time crossers were allowed to capture any passengers they could find who'd crossed at other times. High-ranking seamen judged farcical beauty contests where men dressed up as women, animals, famous pirates. King Neptune and his entourage interrogated first-time crossers. Onlookers cheered and laughed as occasional contrite participants found themselves locked in stocks and pelted with mushy fruit.

The next day, passengers were encouraged to dress up in fancy costumes. Some of us simply wore our own outfits turned inside out or back to front. Others raided the costume shop on the upper deck. The young woman who looked after the children's playroom made sure all her charges were suitably decorated. Joseph was excited to be a seagull. He squawked and whistled but the bright yellow beak and long tail feathers were prohibitive.

All first-time crossers received a certificate declaring their new status. After the hilarity of this, a sudden sadness came over me. Now we were in the great southland.

Elsie found me in a corner seat of the dining room. Joseph slept peacefully on a rug at my feet.

'Well now, Caitlin, what are you doin' sittin' here all alone? And such a sad look on your face.'

'I'm fine, Elsie, I was just thinking about England and Kate and Patrick. I miss them.'

'Who is Kate?'

'She was Patrick's mother, Joseph's grandmother. She died. She took me in after my parents were killed in a train crash. I miss her. I miss her two daughters, Bridie and Molly.'

'Of course you do. And you'll miss them all the days of the life that's left to you. But a new door is opening for you and your wee son. None of us know what the future will bring to us, so best ye keep an open mind and heart. That's what I think. Now come and have a bedtime cup o' tea with me.'

'I don't want to disturb Joseph. See you in the morning, Elsie, and thanks for your kindness.' I watched her move away to find Jack.

That night, I lay awake waiting for slumber to reach me. I thought again about all the people who were no longer in my life. My parents, Kate, Patrick. All dead. Bridie and Molly still alive but far away and untouchable. No more kitchen table talks about the latest Eliot poem, drop-waist dresses or plans for outings. I felt alone and vulnerable.

I dreamt about my mother that night. Images of her flashed in my mind but she had Kate's face. She was braiding my hair, and crooning a lullaby. 'Close your eyes now and rest…the sky's stars are bright.'

I woke up to the touch of Joseph's hand stroking my hair.

60

Caitlin

One morning when I was at my wit's end with prickly heat from a hot stifling wind, I reached the dining room and noticed that there were no officers around. The library and other public rooms were empty.

Elsie had a worried look on her face. 'There's something odd going on around here, I'll be right back.' She scuttled out the door. She came back with the news that the ship was headed into a typhoon and all passengers were ordered to stay in their berths in their respective cabins until the danger was over.

A sense of awe filled the air. All life seemed suspended. I shivered. All my thoughts lost their coherence.

I raced to the playroom to get Joseph. Extra pillows and bedding had been delivered to our cabin and a young crew member arrived to show me how to use them to protect us in the coming weather event. He rolled blankets and covered them with sheets with one long side tucked into the back of the bunk. He put a long blanket around Joseph. All I could see was his face. The sailor put him against the bulkhead. Joseph thought this was a fun game and giggled his way through the process.

The young man insisted that I lie on the same bunk and do the best I could to protect myself with the remaining bedding. The thought of Joseph being tossed out of his cocoon worried me and I edged in beside him. We sang the 'Ali Bali Bee' song, 'The Grand Old Duke of York' and 'Wooloomooloo' until we were hoarse. All the time making sure Joseph's protective blankets kept him covered.

The noise started with a low deep whistle, changing to a moan like a herd of cows lowing. The sound became the roar of a great convoy of army trucks travelling over gravel. I'd never heard anything like it before. My suitcase clattered to the floor from the top of the cupboard then slid again from one end of the cabin to the other, bashing against the door then back again to slam against the bulkhead.

There was a great banging of metal against metal as if some temperamental chef was throwing pots and pans about. I heard shouting but couldn't make any sense of the words.

The ship lifted then plum- meted, throwing me on top of Joseph. He didn't stir. I found a grip on the side of the bunk for both hands and held on tight while making sure Joseph had enough breathing space.

My face was wet with perspiration and contorted with fear. I didn't want us to die on a ship in the middle of the Indian Ocean. I heard great roaring as if some kind of monster was getting ready to gobble up the ship and all on it.

I lost all track of time, place and surroundings. The furore lasted some hours.

The sound of someone knocking on our cabin door was a godsend. There was residual noise from the storm but I managed to convey that we were still alive and thanked the person for his concern. Later, I heard that the storm had fallen short of typhoon status.

At Capetown, I received a letter from Bridie telling me that she and Kevin had got engaged and that she'd decided to return to the house at Langley. Maeve was being too difficult and too involved in the tribal fighting that plagued Ireland. A short letter from Harry in the same mail cheered me up.

Dear Caitlin

By now you'll be on the high seas and I hope the green devil (seasickness) decides to leave you in peace. You're coming closer to me, m'dear, and I'm impatient to see you and to begin our life together. I hope Joseph is well and keeping you entertained. My mother has spread the news of your arrival throughout the town, so be prepared for meeting people who already know you. See you soon. I like that so much I'll say it again: SEE YOU SOON.

Love to you and to Joseph.

Hoo roo!

Harry

The voyage took thirty-seven days and as we approached Australia, I noticed flocks of seagulls gathering. They circled the ship and Joseph waved his arms and yelled, 'Go away.' They ignored him. The seabirds here were an icy white, contrasting with the fat grey birds that swooped along the coasts of England. The winter clothes we'd worn when leaving England were carefully stowed in suitcases. Summer cotton was as much as my hot sweaty body could bear. I learned that the best times to have a walk around the deck was after dinner in the evening or at first light in the morning while Joseph slept.

On the day we landed at Fremantle, I received a lovely surprise. A telegram from Harry: 'Welcome to Australia darling. Longing to see you.' I smiled at the formal language and guessed that he'd had advice about the ship's arrival. We were allowed to get off the ship to say goodbye to Siobhan and Sean, who slipped a note into my hand with a contact address. Elsie, Jack, Joseph and I strolled around the dockside area. I staggered rather than strolled. My legs felt like they were made of jelly. The city felt alien. No castles or cathedrals. Where was the history?

The heat was oppressive the voices strange. I was grateful for the company of Elsie and Jack. We found a little corner shop and sat on the lawn outside licking ice creams. Hundreds of seagulls flapped and squawked above us like an army of parasites searching for prey.

Joseph had a great time chasing the few that landed on the grass beside us. 'Whoosh!' he yelled while clapping his hands, and his treat melted and ran down my hands.

The next and last part of the journey took us across the Great Australian Bight. Not far from the coast of South Australia, we watched dolphins leaping and diving like great shiny salty creatures.

61

Caitlin

Arrival at the Port of Melbourne. Baggage arranged alphabetically waited on the docks for passengers. Crewmen shouted instructions. The banging and crashing of cargo echoed the sounds that were around us when we'd left England. I stood at the rail, watching people move like regimented battalions of ants with a purpose. Sweat shone on shoulders and foreheads as wharfies continued unloading labelled luggage. Shirts and blue singlets were drenched and cigarettes dangled from more than a few lips. The heat made everything warp and my eyes took a long time to adjust to the glare of the sun. Paving and metal and glass waved like underwater mirages. Most unnerving was the knowledge that England and all I'd ever known was so very far away. At some level, this alienation was exciting. Hopeful. Adventurous. I fingered the medal I'd taken from around Pat's neck the night he died and for a moment I felt strength from it pour into my veins.

I searched the dockside for a man who would look like Harry. I thought maybe we wouldn't recognise each other and when I heard the Australian voices around me, I thought I'd never make sense of any conversation. Then I saw him. It was the smile I saw. Wide and happy, and I could almost see the glint in his eyes. He wore a light beige-coloured suit, a white shirt with a stiff collar. His hair was slicked either side of a middle parting. He stood out amongst the dark suits of arriving men and dockworkers clothing. Nothing else mattered. He was here and Joseph and I had survived. I watched his reaction when he spotted us. He jumped and waved his arms high. Then he started pacing and waving. I couldn't hear him above the noise around me but it looked to me as if he was laughing with sheer joy.

At last we were allowed to leave the ship.

Joseph ran ahead of me shouting, 'C'mon, Mummy, c'mon.'

We made it through an obstacle course of barrels and bundles to Harry's side. He herded Joseph and me to a quiet space beyond the piles of ropes, stacks of boxes and lines of landed luggage. Our tea chests and heavy trunks were assigned to one of the carriers that waited dockside for the business. I found the bags and suitcases we'd need for the first week or two. Harry picked them up as if they were full of candy floss, and put them in a corner.

We stood among the smells and crowds and noise of disembarkation, looking into each other's eyes. His eyes were so big and so blue I couldn't see the rest of his face. His grin was wide and his hands were comforting. He cupped both my hands in both of his. Joseph clung to my skirt. My clothes were sticking to me as if I'd been dipped in a warm sea. I wanted to take my hat and coat off and throw them away. Joseph kept looking at Harry with a question on his puzzled face. It had the expression of a wise old farmer studying clouds to determine imminent weather.

Harry looked down at him then knelt to Joseph's height. 'How are ye', young fella?'

Joseph looked at me as if to ask what he should do next.

Harry took a model train from his pocket. 'Would you like this, Joseph? We'll be going on a bigger train very soon.'

My son smiled at him and said, 'Thank you.'

Harry and I laughed. I remembered Kate telling me that laughter between two people is sometimes a closer act of love than any other. In that moment, I knew we'd be all right with Harry. I asked myself if this was love. Whatever it was, I felt weak with it. Harry put his hands either side of my face and softly stroked, then he moved escaping wisps of hair around my ears and at last, he took all of me in his arms. We stood there just breathing each other's smell and knowing this was a good, good place to be.

Since Harry and I started corresponding, my eyes had been hungry for his face, his hands. Now that hunger stayed with me as we went through the fracas of settling luggage and ourselves in the car that would take us to a nearby hotel.

'You look like you could use a cool drink, Caitlin. The nearest cool spot isn't far away but first we'll drop your luggage off at the railway station. We'll be there in a couple of shakes of a rat's tail.'

The newness of his voice surprised and pleased me.

Joseph piped up. 'We thaw lotth of ratth on the ship.'

'Did you now? What colour? Were they black or grey rats, Joey?'

'I think they were black.'

'Well now, Joey, black rats are the harmless breed. It's the grey type we need to be wary of.'

'What doth wary mean?'

'Well now, it means to be careful of something.'

When we reached the hotel, Harry helped Joseph up to his chair then stood tall asking me what I'd like to drink. It seemed to me as if serious formality laced through our attempts at humour.

I don't remember much of the hotel except that ceiling fans and cool drinks helped to take the bite out of the heat. I took my hat and coat off and relaxed. The floor was carpeted and sound was muted. Around the base of the bar a brass foot rail shone like gold. While Joseph and I sipped lemonade, Harry had a beer.

'I can't believe I'm sitting here beside you, in Australia. It's some kind of miracle, I think,' I whispered across a polished wood table.

'And so it is, m'dear. I can't believe the most beautiful face I've ever seen, is right here, right now, beside me. For such a long while I thought of you, and it took a lot of courage to put my thoughts into writing. But I know it's right and I'll do everything in my power to keep you happy. For now, I think it would be grand to take a walk around the botanic gardens. We'll get a cab. There's a restaurant there. Air-conditioned. Nice food. Would you like that?'

I watched his eyes sparkle while he spread out his plans for us, and a ghostly line from Yeats passed through the conversation like a mist:

I have spread my dreams under your feet,
Tread softly because you tread on my dreams.

'We'll catch the four o'clock train. We change trains for Numurkah at Seymour, where a light meal has been arranged. We can pick up refreshments at Shepparton if we feel like it. Then full steam ahead for home. We'll be in Numurkah nine-thirty tonight.'

From dreams to trains in one breath. I liked his practicality.

'It seems everything's in order, Harry. Joseph will probably be asleep by the time we arrive. Now, where's that restaurant and those cool trees?'

'Mummy, I don't want to thleep. I want to hear the train. I want to…'

His eyes began to close. I reached into my bag and brought Milton out and he wrapped his fingers around it. Harry picked him up and, just like a family, we left the hotel and set our course for the gardens.

The restaurant room had high ceilings and fans lazily circulating the air. We were directed to a table by a window that looked out to a pond showing giant lily pads. A table was set with a bottle of wine and two glasses beside a platter of cheese and fruit. Joseph sunk onto the floor. Harry opened the bottle of wine.

'Will he sleep for long?'

'About an hour.'

Harry fiddled with his tie. He ran his fingers through his hair. He stood up. 'There's a heap of stuff we need to talk about, Caitlin. Like where will we live, will you keep up your Red Cross work? Hell! I don't even know what you like to eat.'

'Well, Harry, we're grown-up people. We'll tackle each question as it arises. Let's just sit here and enjoy the time while Joseph sleeps. It might be a while before we're alone again.'

'Well, m'dear, d'ye mind if I take my jacket off and loosen my tie?

62

Caitlin

Numurkah was the penultimate stop on the line and when the train pulled out from Shepparton, Harry started pacing. He walked three steps one way then the same back.

After many trips back and forth, he sat beside me. 'Caitlin, I'm full to the gills with hope for our life here.' He put his arms around me and held me tight.

As the train lurched around the last long curve on the line, he gave a deep, deep sigh and hugged me tight. 'You ready?'

'I am.'

The train slowed and pulled into the station.

We arrived weary and in desperate need of a good wash and change of clothes.

Harry's mother stood back from me, searching my face. She smiled and took my hand. 'Welcome to Australia, Caitlin. Welcome to Numurkah. It's a real treat to see you at last. Harry, dae ye mind the last time we stood on this platform thegither? Dae ye mind how ye picked me up and twirled me around and a'body cheered?'

Harry stopped fussing with luggage and looked at his mother. 'I do that, Ma. So where's the flags and banners and officials that were here on that day?'

'It's like this, Harry: I wanted Caitlin a' tae myself. Didnae want a toon full o' nosey folk at a time like this.'

She fired questions at me. 'How was the ship, Caitlin? Did Joseph sleep at night? Are you hungry?'

She turned to Joseph. 'Well, hello, Joseph. I'm very happy to meet you.'

She picked up a suitcase almost the size of herself.

Harry said, 'Leave that, Ma. I'll get it'

She laughed and took Joseph's hand. 'C'mon, now, we'll have a nice cup o' tea and a long blether. 'Do you like pancakes, Joseph?'

In no time at all, Joseph was asleep in a little bed she'd made ready for him. I rummaged through my suitcase for a clean skirt, blouse and underwear and, after a good wash, I felt almost human.

It was decided that Joseph and I would stay at Lettie's overnight and go to the cottage next morning. Lettie kept herself busy inside while Harry and I sat outside on the back veranda talking until my eyes refused to stay open. The hunger I felt when I first saw him on arrival became intense. He took my arm and we stole away to the fruit trees at the back of the yard.

He grabbed my hands and held them close to his heart. He stroked my face. His eyes filled with tears. He touched his soft lips to mine. The taste and warmth of that first long, long kiss will stay with me through all our challenges for all time. The power of it nearly brought me to my knees.

We held each other close until Harry whispered, 'I know you're dead tired, Caitlin, and there'll be years and years of kissing ahead of us.'

We parted at the kitchen door. I went inside to find Lettie. I heard her talking before her body emerged from the bedroom I'd been assigned.

'Well now, Caitlin, I've put a pile of clean towels on the tallboy for you. They're the fattest, fluffiest towels I could find in Shepparton. There're a few toiletries in the bathroom for you and if I've missed anything or you need anything else, let me know. Now may the sleep gods look kindly on you. I'll see you in the mornin'.' She gave me a big hug then she pulled away from me and stared at my face. She looked straight into my eyes. She took both my hands in hers. 'I'm very, very happy tae meet ye, Caitlin. An' I dinnae think there'll be too many obstacles between us. I'll dae everything possible tae make your life and wee Joseph's life happy and comfortable. Now on ye go before the tears o' welcome start.'

*

I woke up to an unfamiliar bird sound. When I pulled the curtains apart, the sky was silvery grey with a pink tinge on the horizon and I figured that must be east. I sat and watched the sky turn bright orange, then red and I wondered if that colour in the morning prophesied stormy weather as it did in the northern hemisphere.

A good stretch and some deep breathing helped my body to wake up. Apart from the warbling birds, everything was silent. My parched throat demanded succour. I tiptoed in the semi-dark to the kitchen and filled a tall glass of water. Glancing out the window to the side garden, I saw a shadow. Tall, slim build and messy hair that seemed to be standing on end. Harry. The temptation to step outside overpowered any concern for honour and, in slippered feet and thin nightdress, I crept up behind him.

Without turning his head, he murmured, 'I was hoping you'd wake early.'

I leaned into his back and put my head between his shoulder blades. Then ever so slowly, he turned around and we were in each other's arms. It was an extraordinary feeling of homecoming.

'You will never know how happy you've made me, Caitlin, m'darling. When will you marry me?'

'I'd do that tomorrow but first we have things to talk about.'

'What things?'

'Where? What church? Will it be in a church?

'Well, in that case, they'll have to be discussed sensibly over a good country breakfast. Let me cook you some bacon, eggs and tomatoes with Ma's homemade bread. The eggs are from our chooks that you and Joseph will meet later, and the tomatoes are from our garden. Unfortunately, we don't have a pig, so the bacon is from Alec Kinnaird.'

'Is he a friend of yours?'

'Well, kinda – he's the local butcher and you need to keep pally with 'im.'

Over breakfast, I learned that the waking birds were magpies.

63

Caitlin

We spent two days inspecting the Quinn Street property. Harry had made lists of jobs that needed work. The kitchen stove was covered in bird droppings and most of the wooden floors were warped. Damp wallpaper hung from the corners in each room. Outside, a large circle of rocks had a centrepiece of a marble boy-god showing green patches of verdigris from his head to his feet. Joseph inspected the statue from top to bottom.

'Itth got no clothe on, Mummy. It'th rude and itth shoeth are green.'

Harry steered him away to the back of the house, where patches of high grass and herbs gone to seed climbed over the pathways. Silver birch trees defined the property borders. I caught the scent of rosemary, and moved some weeds away from a lovely healthy patch of thyme.

'We could buy this place, Harry. It does have potential.'

'You think so? To make it liveable would mean a lot of hard work, and use up a heap of our savings. We'll give it some thought and talk about it later."

At dinner that night after Joseph was in bed, we put the options on the table. We talked about buying the cottage, improving it and selling at a profit. Lettie thought it would be best to save our assets until a better proposition came along. In the end, we decided to live with Lettie and put plans about the cottage on hold.

'It'll take ye time tae settle in, Caitlin. Best ye get tae know Numurkah and the people in it. Ye might want tae join a club, get a wee job, and ye'll be spendin' a lot o' time wi' the bairn – he's got adjusting to do, same as yersel. Noo, let's talk aboot the weddin' – this is the maist excitin' thing tae happen since Harry got home.'

Lettie's idea was a lavish celebration in a hotel with a four-course meal and a quartet of musicians. We weren't so sure.

'That'll be just fine and dandy, Caitlin. I feel so excited – wish the day would get a move on.'

Here, in this house, Sunday morning was the best time of the week. A leisurely breakfast of bacon, eggs and Lettie's tasty potato scones, with freshly squeezed orange juice and more than one pot of tea.

'So now, you two. When is the wedding going to be, eh?'

'We don't yet know that, Ma. We'll let you know as soon as we do. It will be as soon as we can get it organised. Right now, Caitlin and I are off for a walk. We'll look at the two churches in town and at the registry office. Okay, Joey boy, find your hat. We are going to explore.'

Joseph jumped to Harry's side, excited, like a young puppy.

Lettie said, 'On ye go then. Be back for lunch will you? Caitlin, if you stop in at St John's, say one for an old Scottish excommunicant.'

There was no bitterness in Lettie's mien. She'd said to me earlier, 'I've just grown tired of the God thing, Caitlin. Too much misery in the world. Look at Northern Ireland in the name o' religion. Besides, what more spiritual sustenance can be got outside of a garden and a happy home?'

I saw sincerity in her face. I too had grown tired of the God thing.

'We won't be going that far, Ma, maybe along the river – show the wee fella where I spent a lot o' my young life.'

Lettie took me aside. She whispered, 'Caitlin, if at any time ye feel the need to say an Ave or bless yourself, ye dinnae need tae move away tae a corner where you think naebody sees you. It's all part o' you…bless you.'

I explained to Lettie that it wasn't so much that I felt the strings of my old faith pulling at me, it was more like the rituals I'd learned were so fully ingrained they jumped to the front of my mind at times. My responses to unfamiliar situations brought out reactions like blessing myself. Sometimes it helps to say, 'Holy mother of Jesus' like Pat's mother used to say. Sometimes I pleaded with my lost saints like St Anthony or St Jude to give me wisdom or find some lost thing, to help me unravel the mysteries of this new life. It was only leftover religion.

Lettie put her arms around me. 'I struggled with Catholicism for years, Caitlin, until I realised that it's a religion that takes a scene of capital punishment for its central image and I could no longer support that system. Now I don't want to influence you in any way. Just be yourself in this.'

I still sat with Joseph each night before he went to sleep while he listed his blessings for his two families. 'Bleth Molly and Bridie,' he'd lisp, then he'd add 'Bleth Ireland,' just like Kate had asked him to the last time he'd heard her voice. He'd bless Harry and Lettie and tears would fill my eyes when he'd finish with, 'And God, would you tell my daddy that…' and he'd mention something he'd done that day.

While we walked and sat by the river, we hammered out our plans for our wedding.

'Ma would like a big party. What do you think of that?' Harry murmured with a smile and crinkly eyes, looking into mine.

'I don't mind really, if your ma wants to invite a few of her friends, but I'd prefer a discreet service in a registrar's office, then lunch at home. What about witnesses?' I whispered.'

'What about a honeymoon?' he countered, and pulled me closer.

Joseph got bored gathering the green peppercorns scattered around the tree and tried his skill at skipping stones the way Harry had shown him.

Reluctantly prising ourselves apart, we got to our feet and walked towards home.

Lettie stood by the gate when we turned into our (our!) street. 'Thoct ye'd eloped and I'd missed the feast. It's nice tae see ye back hame.'

With Joseph between us and looking up to both of us in turn, Harry and I giggled like a pair of truants.

64

Caitlin

My Australian vocabulary grew. I especially liked 'ear-bashing' and 'bludge'. Other words had me flummoxed: 'chiacking', 'yootelemluv'. And 'bastard', I was told, was an endearment!

Little by little, I have adjusted to a foreign way of doing things, and am now locked into domestic infinities between Lettie and myself. Now and again, I take out Patrick's notebooks and letters. I am grateful that he wrote so much down. I revere these records – not only because they are his words; they also help me keep a bond with what had been our life and will connect my son to that life, however tenuous the link may become. It is also a connection for Harry to his wartime friend. I hope Harry will understand that when he finds me touching the lines and tracing the curves and forms of the words.

One morning morning after Harry had gone to work, I peeked into his bedroom. It was a small space at the rear end of the house. It held a single bed, a chest of drawers with a mirror above it and a chair; the style you'd normally see in a dining room. Harry had only used the room for sleep. No decorations or pictures or frippery cluttered the walls or furniture. When Harry wanted to be alone, the garden, the shed or the river was where he sought his privacy. The bed was tidy and flat with the corners of a patchwork quilt tucked neatly under the mattress. A shirt that I remembered seeing him wear hung on a corner of the iron bedstead, and on the dresser there was a brass-handled hairbrush. When I caught the scent of maleness that filled the room, I had the urge to be near him, to be held in his strong arms and hear whispered love. It was a good thing Lettie couldn't see the expression on my face – eyes half-closed and lips parted. Waiting. Wanting.

Later that night after Lettie had gone to a meeting at the Caledonian Society, I asked Harry to come with me. Got something to show you,' I whispered in his ear.

'Ooh, a surprise,' he chortled, and followed me to his old room.

'I think this would be a great room for Joseph. What do you think of that? We could paint it and put new curtains and…' I didn't get to say another word.

Harry lifted me up and placed me full length on the bed. In a deep hoarse voice, he croaked, 'This is where I dreamt of you, Caitlin. Wanted you. And now, here you are. Can't believe it. Pinch me, Caitlin.'

'I'd rather kiss you.' I ran my fingers over his brow, his lips, his chin. 'You have a perfect profile. If I were a sculptor, I'd make a bust of your head. And we'd place it on a little polished table at the end of the hallway and it would be the first thing we, and visitors, would see when entering our home.'

Harry smiled through soft laughter. 'Caitlin, you will never know what you have given me with your presence in my life.'

And so we spent the next while together with the colours and scents of Harry's growing-up years. The sound of the front door opening and a loud 'Hello' from Lettie jolted us back to reality.

<h1 style="text-align:center">65</h1>

<h1 style="text-align:center">Caitlin</h1>

During the voyage to Australia, Joseph had sometimes cried at night time. Here, at Harry's house, these episodes became a thing of the past. Hearing his laughter, I was confident that we had the foundation for a sustainable happy life together.

One morning, I was in the bedroom at the back of the house folding linen. I stopped to pick up a fluffy raggedy soft dog. It had long brown ears and tiny brown tail, black button eyes and nose. I held it close and smelled it and stroked it. Patrick had bought it for our baby. He'd named it Milton after his poet hero. The day he gave it to me was the last day of our honeymoon – the day before Kate, Bridie and Molly were due to return from Rathdrum.

We'd been looking in a toyshop window. I'd moved to the hat shop next door and heard the tinkle of a doorbell. Later, when we were sitting rugged up on the garden bench watching the sunset, Patrick signalled that I should put my hand into his pocket.

I asked, 'Why?'

He stuttered something that sounded like 'babby,' pulled my hand and shoved it inside his coat pocket.

I felt paper covering something soft. 'What is it?'

He shrugged. I pulled out a crumpled paper bag. Sticking from the top was the loveliest of faces – it looked real, like it had once been a living thing – now stuffed with the softest cotton. Joseph had slept with it every night since his birth. And when he learned to hold it, his hands lay still around it through sleep and dreams.

The other night he'd announced that he was a big boy now and didn't need Milton but when I checked after he'd fallen asleep, Milton was cuddled up close to him as he'd always been.

66

Caitlin

By mid-day on our wedding day, the temperature had reached a hundred degrees. Or, as Harry said, a century. The young priest had a dilemma about our request to be married in the vestry of the church, a compromise for a fallen Catholic and a non-believer. Although Harry had said he'd convert to Catholicism to please me, I told him I liked him as he was. Conversion was not a good idea. My Catholic faith had been mostly battered out of me by life, but I felt that getting married in a sanctified place strengthened the vows we'd make. Also, the only formal faith I understood would be good for Joseph until he was old enough to form his own belief system. Lettie didn't mind one way or another. I'd heard her say, 'Each to their own when it comes to dogma.'

The ceiling fans in the church laboured to keep the air flowing and Lettie slipped a hanky sprinkled with eau de cologne into my hand as she and Joseph escorted me slowly down the aisle. The blue shade of my suit matched the blue of the sky above us and a little white lace hat tilted jauntily to one side completed my outfit. I carried a small bouquet of flowers and fern from the garden. Harry stood by the vestry door. As our eyes connected, he winked and grinned with the gladness of a child who'd taken part in a competition and won. He took a breath so deep it stretched the front of his jacket.

I had the feeling that the priest rushed us through the formalities as if his superior (or God) was watching and disapproved of this 'half-baked' ceremony. He ended the proceedings by whispering, 'I give you my blessing for a long and happy life.'

Mrs Coffey and Harry's friend Dave were our witnesses. Joseph was dressed in a little sailor suit that Bridie had bought for him. The top was trimmed with navy blue stripes. Lettie had ironed the white pants in the style of a real sailor – five crossway folds on the legs. He sat still beside her while she whispered little stories about the icons on the walls and the inscriptions on the stained-glass windows. As we left the vestry, there were hugs kisses smiles and more than a few tears from these two loving supporters of our union. The three of us walked hand in hand down the aisle. Dave linked arms with Lettie and Mrs Coffey and followed us. We gazed and grinned at each other as if we'd conquered all two hundred Scottish Munros. Harry linked one of my arms into one of his. It was all I needed to stabilise my shaking body. I brought my face level with his and we stood there, still, safe and together.

A few parishioners sitting in the back of the nave stood as we drew near. An image of Kate flashed before my eyes and I felt tears gathering.

An elderly woman handed me a little posy of flowers and said, 'God bless you.' Her aged face smiled.

Lettie whispered, 'That's Bert Wotherspoon's granny. She brought him up and I think she'd gie the world tae see Bert wi' a lovely partner like you, Caitlin.'

The smell of summer and the blinding colours of blossoms were everywhere. Blue and white agapanthus, roses grouped in colours of red, next to white next to yellow, and further back against the boundary fence, rows of white, gold and lavender hibiscus.

Joseph bent to pick up a rock. 'Look, Harry, it'th a thtone teddy bear.' His excitement made Harry hoot with laughter.

'See, Joseph, it looks like it's lying in the sun. Its legs are pointing to the sky.'

Quick as a flash, Joseph turned it around. 'Look, Harry, now it'th crawling.'

Happiness and sun and flowers were all around us. I felt blest.

Joseph wanted to spend time searching for more rocky creatures but a promise of sweets was more attractive.

We returned home to a table set with shiny starched linen, crystal glasses and silver platters filled with turkey, beef, a roasted leg of lamb. Dishes of golden roasted potatoes, steamed beans, carrots and parsnips, all homegrown, sat between the meats. Along the edges of the table were small china dishes filled with chutney, cranberry sauce and a selection of mustards. An iced fruitcake, decorated with flowers from the garden, waited on the sideboard, making a lovely sweet addition to the feast.

In this room of peacock feathers in tall green vases, and an ornately framed print of Gainsborough's *Cottage Girl*, crockery clinked with cutlery and voices competed with each other to tell stories of past wedding days. Outside, the day's heat pounded like blood pulsing through veins, and Bonza slept unseen in the hallway.

Mrs Coffey bubbled and giggled as she took her place at the table. 'Well, Lettie, you've worked wonders today. I thank you for including me'

'Not at all, Esme. We wouldn't want it any other way,' Lettie said, and passed dishes around.

The meal over, we spent the early afternoon under the apricot tree.

Between bites of wedding cake, Mrs Coffey said, 'For you, Caitlin, I do hope you learn to love this country as much as you love Harry.'

Joseph's chatter slowed and his eyelids began to droop.

Harry bent to pick him up, 'Time to put the boy down for a sleep.' He winked at me. A conspiratorial smile tweaked the edges of his lips.

We had decided we'd have our honeymoon trip to the high country in winter, where we'd have fun in the snow. This would give Joseph time to get to know his new home. Lettie announced that she and Esme were off to an open garden event and wouldn't be home until very late.

Later when we were lying side by side, resting from the heat of the afternoon, and our bodies not touching except he had my hand lightly cupped in his, I heard the universe sing.

67

Caitlin

Harry's deep drawling voice filtered through the branches of the fig tree, and touched my ears like a warm hug. Now and again, Joseph interrupted with excited questions. I couldn't make out the exact words but I had the feeling that Harry was explaining something to him. The conversation was punctuated with childlike giggles and an occasional guffaw from Harry. I moved the basket of beans and empty bowls away from the table, where I'd been sitting for the past half-hour, to a ledge in front of the kitchen window. Now, I was out of sight but could see and hear them distinctly.

Joseph sat cross-legged on a grassy patch, his nose and cheekbones white with zinc cream, and a too-big floppy linen hat, a copy of the one on Harry's head, covered his blue-black curls. Earlier, Harry had given him a lesson on the dangers of the Australian sun while he'd smeared his own face and neck.

I wondered about Harry's obsession with skin care. I thought he'd have been weathered to his native climate. Then I remembered: in one of his letters he said he'd been badly burned and hospitalised.

So there they were. The child and his teacher either side of a red-painted four-wheeled bogie, or billycart as they call it here.

A long straight plank of jarrah wood, sided by shorter slats of pine stencilled with markings, showed an earlier life as an orange crate. One end of the central plank was fitted with a padded red, feather-patterned brocade cushion studded with brass thumbtacks. Two large wheels at this end looked like they'd once belonged to a baby's pram. From this, the contraption sloped away to a metal axle fixed to two smaller wheels. A sturdy white rope attached to the axle was the steering mechanism.

A week before, I'd found Harry rummaging through the shed. He whistled while he shifted boxes and garden tools and bits of machinery. Finally a loud 'Eureka' signalled that his search was successful. To me, it looked like a mass of rusty metal, buckled wheels and warped wood. Harry's expression mirrored the exultant joy on Joseph's face; like that of a young child who'd tasted ice cream for the first time.

'Is that what the racket has been about? What in heaven's name is it?' I asked.

'Joseph's Christmas present.' He looked at the downward tilt my mouth had taken. 'Aw, don't look like that, love… Wait till you see what this'll look like by Christmas Eve… Trust me.'

I saw an earnest, anxious to please expression in his face. Like a child trying to please a parent.

Now, as I looked through the window on this hot Christmas morning and watched pure undiluted happiness spread over Joseph's face, I knew that I'd never again doubt Harry's ability to look after us. The spokes on the wheels sparkled. He'd painted the rims white and polished the middle plank until it shone burnished in the sun. From where I stood, I could see the rings and whorls on the wood.

'Now, Joe, y'see this part? This is what guides the wheels,' he explained, pointing to the moving part of the axle. 'And see, if you take the rope in both hands like this,' he demonstrated, his large sun-browned hands covering Joseph's tiny white fingers. 'Now pull with your right hand.'

Joseph watched the movement of the wheels. His mouth opened wide.

'Now pull with your left hand.'

He pulled again and looked up to Harry as if he was looking at God himself.

'Well done, Joseph boy – you'll make a great driver.'

Joseph giggled.

'Now, Joey, this is the most important bit here,' Harry said, taking hold of a stick attached to the left side of the cart.

'What ith it?' the tiny voice asked.

'This is the brake. What d'you think you use it for?'

He shrugged.

'Look at it, Joe. D'ye see where it's close to? Take hold of it and pull it towards the back.'

Joseph studied the stick. He took in his left hand and pulled it backwards. 'It'th thtuck onto the wheel,' he squealed.

'Yup, you got it. Now can you tell me what it's used for?'

'Ith it to make the cart thtop?'

'Got it in one!' Harry shouted, slapping Joseph on the back. 'Now you're ready to sit on it."

Joseph climbed on. He sat like a champion. Back straight, looking ahead. He took hold of the rope handle as if he was holding a horse's bridle.

At that moment, Lettie appeared from the back garden carrying a basket of peaches. 'I hope you're no' lettin' him oot on the street in that thing,' she said to Harry.

'Not t'day, Ma, this is just to get him familiar wi' the workings o' it.' Harry took the rope from Joseph, saying, 'Let's go for a wee ride aroun' the yard.'

Joseph held onto the sides and let himself be wheeled around the garden all the while shouting, 'Eeehah!' and 'Yippeee!'

At one-point, Harry stopped and gazed into the distance. He looked towards the river. I had the feeling that he was listening for another voice – seeing another time.

Joseph called to him, 'Harry, why did you thtop?'

Harry roused himself, turned to his charge and grinned. He looked up, saw Lettie and me at the window, and waved. In that blessed sun-filled moment, my heart beat a loud, long tattoo for him.

Lettie, taking the empty bean basket said, 'I dinnae ken the last time Harry looked so happy, Caitlin, an' it's all thanks to you and Joseph.'

'Well, Lettie, I've never seen my boy so happy and it's all thanks to your boy.'

We laughed at each other. I put the kettle on the hob and she called out to the yard, 'Kettle's on, boys… Time for a break!'

It puzzled me that there was no sign of the spirit of Harry's father in this house – like he'd never existed. And as I looked at the shining joy on the faces of my menfolk – two fatherless creatures – being all things to each other through play and laughter. I wondered if this was a karmic reward for past pain.

68

Caitlin

When Joseph and I walked along the main street of Numurkah, heads turned and I sensed whispers and nods from the locals. Now and again, when we stood in line at the butchers or general store, reassurance came with a friendly smile or quiet 'g'day'. My son's quick smile and wide-eyed scanning of the big glass jars filled with sweets at the corner shop endeared him to the storekeepers and customers. He learned very quickly to ask for 'lollies'.

The first time I heard, 'Hello, Caitlin. Settled in yet?' from a neighbour woman, I wanted to cry. I'd had such a longing for green fields and crocuses and soft rain, this simple kindness overwhelmed me.

When I told Lettie about these feelings, she said, 'Och, dearie me, I missed the hills of Scotland. I missed the rain. I missed the voices and the songs. I used to go in to shops, not to buy anything, but to search for the sound of a familiar voice. Caitlin, you need a good long greet! I mind how it was when I came here as a young lassie. So it's all right to find yourself a quiet corner and weep a while. You'll feel the better for it.'

The street names of Numurkah told stories of old emigrants who'd made their mark with the local government or had been successful with business ventures. Wealth here had been created from hard work on sheep and beef farms and countryside lush with fruit.

One morning soon after my arrival, when the sun had barely risen over the top edge of the backyard fence, I crept out in my nightie and bare feet while everyone was asleep. The smell of ripe apricots lured me towards their source. The branches hung so low with the weight of its bounty, they nearly touched the ground.

Lettie often sat under this tree on an old wicker chair. She called it her ashram. On this pink glorious morning, I sat there for a few minutes with my eyes closed. When I felt something brush the top of my head, I looked up to the fattest ripest apricots like golden orbs of light shining through the greenery. I plucked three. My teeth broke through the skin, juice spurted and ran down my chin and dripped onto the white front of my nightgown, leaving a spreading yellow stain. When I'd finished my feast, I sat back in the chair, closed my eyes and gave myself up to thoughts about this new unfamiliar life I'd chosen.

The morning sun grew warmer. I heard the sound of running water and wandered inside.

'G'day,' Harry said, snuggling his face into my frizzled early morning hair. 'Ready for breakfast?'

69

Caitlin

Harry's house was the oldest house in the town. It had been built in 1875 by the man the street was named after, Henry Meiklejohn, one of the first lawyers to arrive there. Harry's description of the house hadn't really done it justice. Lettie had worked like a Trojan to acquire it and with the help of Harry's army pay she'd discharged the mortgage before he returned from the war. Happiness in this house started at the dark brown front door. The front step gleamed with red cardinal polish that almost hid the dimples and hollows carved with age and footsteps.

My first impression was the scent of lavender mixed with something savoury coming from the kitchen. Then I noticed the shine and glint on things like brass door handles and window fittings. White lace curtains burst out from windows like a song and the vibrant blues and greens of soft furnishings made me want to meld their chorus of colours to the melody humming in my heart.

Most walls were papered in embossed patterns of oversized ferns and flowers. The calcimined kitchen walls shone white between tiers of iron pots and copper moulds that hung from brackets above a giant black stove. A black iron sink was framed in cupboard doors painted red and ochre, in front of a large window that faced east. The floor, covered in varnished slate, showed fine grey and blue-black grains in some spots.

'My mother thinks she's Italian,' Harry murmured to me when I'd commented on the colours.

'Nothin' o' the sort,' Lettie piped up from the door. 'I'm a Scot through and through!'

179

The hallway was the darkest, coolest spot in the house. The walls were lined with prints of manor houses and Scottish mountain scenes like Landseer's *Monarch of the Glen*. Sometimes I'd see Joseph looking up at this picture with a puzzled look on his face, as if he had questions to ask but hadn't quite formed them into words. The picture reminded me of my father; that same print had been on a wall in his study.

Lettie was a tiny thin woman as readable as an open book. You could tell what her next words would sound like by the honesty in her face. She was passionate about learning through books. Each Wednesday afternoon, she'd toddle off to the local library and, an hour or so later, would arrive back excited about the treasures she'd found. While Harry was at war, she'd tackled house maintenance problems with her ingrained Scottish ingenuity. Since he'd come home, she delegated such matters back to him. She protected her soft Celtic skin with slathers of Pond's cream before going outside each morning and before bedtime. She always wore a hat outdoors and her arms were covered even on the hottest days.

Like Kate in faraway Ireland, Lettie lived by certain self-imposed rules. Her favourite, posted on the pantry door: 'Think before you speak, read before you think.'

She quoted it to me and added, 'That's how we achieved full suffrage in 1908, Caitlin. You should have seen us, marching and shouting down the politicians. They had no idea what they were up against. Persistence, Caitlin, that's the way to achieve.'

I understood now what gave Harry the positive spirit we loved. Lettie didn't 'do' housework or sew or cook. She went to war on these things, tackling them with verve and vitality. She had a wiry whalebone body – built on porridge and the rough weather of western Scotland. Her constitution repelled any disease that chose to attack her.

70

Caitlin

Over the coming months, I learned the value of wet hessian over a small wooden cupboard with a wire net door to keep meat fresh. I learned about rising at dawn in summer to get house chores done before the heat of the sun made everything too hot to handle. Even at that hour, Harry's mother insisted I wear a hat when feeding the chooks or hanging out towels that dried in the time it took to put the next lot through the mangle. I learned about the pleasures of plucking a ripe apricot from a laden tree at the back of the yard in mid-February while north winds blew snow on my homeland.

Homeland. In February back there, snowdrops pushed green shoots through frosty ground and in the woodlands the tall beginnings of bluebells began their march to summer glory. In Numurkah, I learned to fear a wind from the north that brought the threat of bushfires.

Harry was helping me clean out the last of the fruit from the apricot tree. 'You're daydreaming again, Caitlin. Wanna tell me what's on your mind?

'It's nothing really…just a feeling that this wind will bring a bushfire and this might be the last apricots we'll ever see.'

He took my basket, took me by the hand and sat both of us down. 'Listen to me, Caitlin, look into my eyes.' His eyes were clear and fearless. 'Do not be frightened, Caitlin. I'll make sure the north wind comes nowhere near our little oasis here. See that track I've been clearing around the house? And the distance between the trees? When we finish pickin' the last of this harvest, I'll clear away all the undergrowth and no self-respecting fire would dare make its presence here. I don't like to see fear in your face. It's a face for reflecting smiles and laughter. Besides, you've battled a lot in your life. You are invincible.'

Lettie had a young woman, Maggie, come in once a week to 'do' for her. Maggie scrubbed floors, changed bedlinen and occasionally made dinner. She helped with fruit picking and jam making. She was a wealth of information about where to buy the best cut of meat, the best shoes, the nicest dresses and who was the best hairdresser. At these weekly meetings with Maggie, I'd insist on sharing a pot of tea with her – a comforting reminder of Kate and Mrs Blainey.

71

Caitlin

Numurkah

Victoria

Australia

February 1923

Dear Bridie

Congratulations to you and to Kevin on your engagement. It is truly exciting news. You must write and tell me about your plans. When and where will your wedding be? What will you wear? I wish I could share this time with you. I've been thinking a lot about England and the fun we had and I ask myself, what am I doing in this strange environment? How did this happen? I feel this journey is leading me home to a life among loving people in an untroubled environment.

There is nothing here that I can compare with my life in England. Here, there are vast tracts of landscape that look empty. Harry tells me that in that vastness there is life hidden beneath the surface. A recent storm brought rain that formed puddles in any hole it could find. Dried-up lakes became a heaven filled with waterbirds, small mammals and insects. Two days after the storm, Harry borrowed his boss's car and took Joseph and me for a tour around the local area. The sun was high in the sky and I was struck dumb by the colours and verdant grass that covered what had been an arid landscape.

If Australia's bugs had been going to kill me, they'd have done it by now. They are many and vicious. Lettie keeps a bottle of vinegar handy on the kitchen bench. She says it's the best antidote for mossie bites, and a headache will disappear when attacked by a vinegar-soaked cloth. She tells Maggie (her helper) to put a capful in water that's used to clean the windows.

Life here presents challenges I haven't faced before, but Harry understands. Everything he gives me is driven by his disciplines from other areas of his life – work and home maintenance. One thing I know: it's not only the pleasure our bodies give to each other, there is also the comfort of like minds. I find it amazing that a lot of the books in this house are similar to those in the house at Langley. Donne's poetry, Thomas Hardy and Dickens are all here. Biographies on politicians, especially Ramsay MacDonald, look like they have been well read. It's no wonder that Harry and Patrick became friends. And this connection reassures me that I have made the right decision.

Bridie, that's all my news for now. It would be lovely to hear from you.

I nearly forgot to tell you that our wedding day was just as we planned. A few guests, a quiet ceremony and a lovely lunch at home. Joseph wore the little sailor suit you bought for him – it now fits perfectly. It feels good and right to be Mrs Harry Kenihan.

Love to you and to Kevin,

From Caitlin, Harry and Joseph

72

Bridie

Langley, Berks
April 1923

Dear Caitlin and Harry

Kevin and I have just been talking about you and I decided it was time I told you that. We do think of you and hope that all is well in your new life. We're thinking about coming to Australia to live. Himself has been to the library to find out more about the country and found all this information about bushfires. Apparently half of the state of Victoria was burnt out and people died along with millions of sheep and countless other animals. Mind you, that was in 1851 and I'm hoping that bushfires have learned to behave by now. Dear God, Caitlin, I do hope you and wee Joseph are safe and that Harry's house is near water.

I have to tell you that Maeve has died – peacefully in her sleep, just like Ma. She has left the cottage to victims of the troubles. I'm hoping that this bequest will bring softness to her soul and make her last journey easier than this life has been for her.

Next news is that Molly and Michael are expecting their second baby come autumn. We meet often and I can tell you that wee Isabella is thriving. She's walking and talking at a mile a minute.

That's all for now, Caitlin. Please know that you are in my thoughts and I will let you know how our plans develop.

Kevin has enclosed a PS – (he has to get a word in).

Well now, Caitlin and Harry.

You know that the ould sod has been locked in a fight for independence that was granted in January 1922 when the Irish Free State was born. But still they fight. Civil war is a terrifying duel. I'm sorry for my people but I will never hold a killing weapon in my hand. As Yeats, said, 'If there is no hatred in a mind, assault and battery from the wind can never tear the linnet from the leaf.'

There's a raging storm of details in my mind but I can't see through the maelstrom. This I do know: I will learn to love Australia, in spite of my Irishness.

Love from Bridie and Kevin

73

Caitlin

When I read Bridie's letter, it was as if the troubles and the bitterness lodged in Maeve's heart were mixed with the songs and laughter of our past life. The sad and the joyful came flying through the air to rest in our Numurkah parlour. Questions about when they would come and where they would stay were overridden by the joy of knowing they would be sharing our life.

Harry found me daydreaming over a tub of soaking linen.

'Where are you, my love?' Harry put his arms around me. 'Come back, m'dear.'

'I was thinking that if the Quinn Street house is still available, it would be perfect for Bridie and Kevin.'

'Depends if they want to stay in Numurkah. I mean, what kind of work would Kevin do here?'

'Well, he's very good at handling horses. He shoes them and grooms them, and I think this town could use his skills.'

Harry stood looking out the window, his mind ticking over. 'Well, m'dear, if you're happy with that, I am too. But first they have to get themselves to Numurkah.'

74

Nina

Garmisch
Southern Germany

Mr Kenihan

Thank you for your letter about your wedding. I wish you great happiness. Thank you also for describing summer to me. It is winter here and the snow is thick and deep on every street. I am thinking I will try to get to Australia before the end of your summer. I will write you the details of my arrival.

Nina Grottenthaler

*

Nina put the letter against the clock on the mantelshelf. She wrapped her favourite woollen scarf round her head and went out to knock on the door of her old neighbou and suddenly remembered that he would never answer her signal, or anyone's signal, ever again.

The latest snowfall over a week ago had been light and melted in a weak winter sun. Usually, the first signs of spring growth in Nina's garden were tiny spear-like blades of green that sprang into healthy patches of white edelweiss bells. If I find signs of early flowers, I will stay. If not, I will go.

She poked gently around with a trowel and drew snow and gravel around the edges but all was brown, black or grey. No lively green showed up.

Once again, Nina pulled on her worn galoshes and ancient padded coat and made her way to the local library. Her steps seemed lighter than at other times when she'd walked this pathway. She had decided, and wanted to share the news with William. *Will he be happy for me? Will he think me insane? How will I get from here to the Antipodes? Where will I find a home?* Thoughts and questions swirled as if there was an eye of a storm in her head.

75

Caitlin

Harry took Joseph for a walk to the nearest tree-free place he could find. He'd made a kite with paper and balsa wood. It had a tail with little white bows made from ribbon he'd pinched from Lettie's work basket.

'Look, Mummy,' Joseph had called out. 'It'th about a mile long!'

'Slight exaggeration there,' Harry whispered to me.

I waved them off with an order to have a good time.

Later that day, the weather had turned unseasonably cool and I was tidying up Joseph's clothes and toys when I heard Lettie's low lilt coming from the living room. I peeped in. Joseph was sitting at her feet. Her hands covered his and rested on her knees.

'When I was a little girl in Scotland,' she said, 'I lived in a house that used to be the local priest's house. It was right in the middle of a swamp and sometimes in winter the nearby river would reach the end of the garden path. My mother'd watched me, the way a hawk watches its young. One day when the river moved back to its regular course, it left behind a bright green satin ribbon entangled in riverside ferns…'

I didn't hear the rest of the story but next time I looked Joseph was snuggled up close to her chest. His mouth was open so that his two front teeth showed over his bottom lip. Two pairs of eyes were closed and the soft breathing of deep sleep came from both of them.

I went outside looking for Harry to show him this wonder. A cold wind swept up the street from the river, lifting tatters of papers and dried crumpled leaves. I found him sitting on the seat of his motorbike. He looked up and I could see he was troubled about something. I found an old sack, placed it on the ground at his feet and settled myself on it. The silence was palpable.

Eventually, he slid down beside me. He put his arms around me. He spoke in a voice I'd never heard before. 'Did Paddy ever tell you about the night we came across the German soldier?

'Well, the notes in the package I sent to you were actually written by me. Pat's hands shook too much, but the words are all his. Why do you ask?'

'It's just that I wrote to the German's mother. Not sure why I did that. Maybe it's to do wi' hoping you'd come here. I decided it would be one way of getting rid of the bad feelings I had about the entire German race after me mate Danny was killed. You and I both know that life is too short for that attitude.'

'Tell me what happened back then.'

'Well, when I saw the German, at first I wanted to kill him and, if it hadn't been for your Patrick, I just might have done that.'

'How did he change your mind?'

'Just the way he talked to me. He said that hatred turns your heart sour and leaves no room for love.'

When he said this, Harry turned away from me. He clenched his jaw tight and his hands at his side took the shape of fists. For a few seconds, darkness settled around him. I wanted to reach out – to touch him.

Then he turned to me and said, 'I've never forgotten those words. Sometimes when I meet up with Mrs Coffey, I think about the German boy's mother, and at one of those times, I made up my mind to write to her.' He pulled a crumpled piece of paper from his pocket and handed it to me. 'This is her answer.'

I saw a single page of German words, attached to a second page of the English translation and written by another hand. The formal language expressed feelings of gratitude and appreciation for Harry's kind gesture and ended by wishing Harry a safe and happy future.

'Well, Harry, it sounds to me that the mothers of this world are building bridges across the hell of war and it's up to you and me to put as much joy as we possibly can into our life together.'

He looked at me as if he was drinking my very soul into his heart. He crumpled in tears. 'Go away, Caitlin. Please.'

Listening to Harry talk about Patrick reminded me of an episode on the ship when Joseph turned his back on an older boy who'd demanded his ice cream. My son didn't say a word, he just stood silent and strong. It pleased me to know that, at that young age, my son was a pacifist.

Minutes later, I heard the sound of Harry's motorbike take off. Lettie must have heard. She came out to stand with me at the shed door. She hooked her left arm around my right arm and we stood together like a bastion of defiance against anything that would threaten to harm our life.

'Where's Joseph?'

'Oh, he's fast asleep still. I laid him on the settee. Harry will be fine, Caitlin.'

I nodded. I understood that this was Harry's way of dealing with bad memories.

'He'll look at the land and count his blessin's. So don't you be worryin' 'bout him.'

The only tune Harry ever whistled was 'When Irish Eyes are Smiling' and when he returned from his bike ride, I could hear his faint rendition coming from the shed. A feeling of contentment embraced me like a soft silk robe.

76

Nina

Nina Grottenthaler stared hard at the contraption in a corner between the kitchen bench and the black cast iron sink. Water dripped from a length of hessian into a metal basin beneath the fabric-covered box. She picked the bottom edge between her right-hand index finger and thumb and lifted it halfway to the top. She was puzzled and surprised to see a small dish filled with butter and a long bottle half-filled with milk. She felt an icy brush on her arm and immediately, her memory spun like an airborne animal back to the ski slopes of Garmisch.

She saw her darling Karl as he was before the war, swooping down mountainsides and dancing over moguls on soft and hard formations, his face hidden under goggles and hat, but Nina knew he'd be smiling with love of the freedom that the hiss and spit of skis on snow gave him.

Nina was shocked into stillness. Her son had no place in this new hell of a land where breathing burned your throat and clothes stuck to your body. Images of Karl faded. She touched a pocket on the right side of her dress where she kept a tiny package of his fine blond, baby hair.

As far as Nina could see the road ahead, it was filled with strange unknowns, like maps of twisted roads, fankled and going nowhere. Linguistic challenges of the past two years were nothing compared to the hazards of building a life in this godforsaken part of the universe.

The discouraged mood fizzled out and Nina considered all that she'd achieved. She'd learned to read, write and speak English to the point where she'd no fear of dealing with officials in the government

193

departments she encountered on her bureaucratic journey from defeated Germany to Shepparton.

She found her notebook and wrote.

I am the architect of my own life. For my brave, dead son, I will build a good life here. I will learn to love this topsy-turvy world where beds of abundant colour edge gardens in January. Where people walk around town in shorts and thin unbuttoned shirts.

With help from my librarian William and the Australian government, I made the journey to Australia.

1. Finding accommodation in Shepparton defied my patience and independence.

2. Conversation in my own language will happen if I get out amongst people.

3. Understanding the strange Australian vernacular will take time. Idioms like 'earbash' and 'bludge' that I hear in shops need translating.

The small radio she kept switched on all her waking hours, helped her get familiar with current political affairs and goods advertised in shops.

When youthful luminous images of Karl confronted her, she'd often say, 'Karl, my boy, you don't belong here. There is no snow here. Stay in Germany, my son.'

Mainly, Nina suffered from chronic astonishment at the new world she found herself in. Sun-scorched paddocks. Wide roads. The abundance of many kinds of fruit. When she arrived at her first home (a rented room in a large bungalow), owned by a widow, she was amazed to see a tree in the yard so loaded with peaches that the branches swept the ground around the base. Her early morning feast of fresh peaches straight from the tree was a luxury. She remembered the touch and taste of that first feast for the rest of her life.

The images faded. The bottle of milk Nina held in her hands felt warm. The air around her was hot and damp. She sat down on an old kitchen chair. With her spine ramrod straight, she rolled her tongue into a tube and began breathing in, long slow cooling breaths. She closed her eyes and indulged in visions of the snow slopes of Garmisch.

Caitlin

On a sunny afternoon, Harry came home from work in the newspaper's horse and buggy. 'Great chance for you and Joseph to see a different stretch of the local area,' he said as he picked Joseph up and tucked him giggling and wriggling under one arm.

'Where are you taking us? And why the horse, not the car?'

'Gotta talk to a bloke over at Nathalia. We could pack a picnic – have lunch under a tree somewhere. When was the last time you and Joey travelled in a horse and buggy?'

'So long ago, I've forgotten what it feels like.'

'There ye go then. A new Australian experience.'

'Can I take my billycart?'

'Not today, Joe boy. The roads are a bit rough. You could bring your kite, though. Don't forget the zinc cream.'

I loved the way Harry dealt with a child's wants by anticipating disappointments and finding an acceptable substitute.

Within minutes, we'd packed our basket with apricots and figs from the garden, with some cheese and bread. Joseph carried the water bag and while I stacked the basket and a blanket in the back of the buggy, Harry showed his young helper how to attach the waterbag to a hook on the side of the buggy.

We rolled along, watching white puffy clouds make shapes of monkeys and elephants and bears. Then as if they'd got tired of their impersonations, they trailed off across the sky like wisps of cotton wool, their day's work done.

We stopped near the entrance to the property of Harry's destination. We spread the blanket under the shade of a huge peppercorn tree at the edge of the road. Joseph ran across to where a fence was hung with clusters of grapes so small I thought they were blackcurrants.

'They're wine grapes,' Harry explained. 'OK to eat.'

I noticed that he never took his eyes off Joseph. As soon as my son stepped on the long grass edging the road and hiding the lower growth of the vines, Harry strode across and took Joseph's hand while scanning the area they stood on.

'Watching for frogs?' I asked when I reached them.

'Well, no. Snakes.'

I screamed, picked Joseph up, dragged him away and, my legs moving like pistons in a well-oiled machine, reached the buggy and almost threw him onto it. Harry stood laughing. He pushed his hat to the back of his head. My hands shook and my knees wobbled with fright.

'What'th the matter, Mummy?'

I couldn't respond. My throat had dried up. My tongue felt like it was made of the gravel beneath our feet.

'Listen, Caitlin, if there'd been any snakes there, they'd be long gone as soon as they sensed we were near them.'

I felt like slapping the grin off his face. 'You didn't warn me about snakes!' I yelled.

He put his arms around me and said to Joseph, 'Come here, Joseph.'

We stood locked in a triptych mixed of fear and Harry's laughter.

While Harry talked to the farmer about establishing a scheme to help local veterans find work, Joseph and I wandered around the house garden talking to the family kelpie and listening to a cockatoo reciting a poem where every second word was 'bloody'.

In the bright day sunlight, beyond the back fence of the house garden, I noticed a low rise a fair distance away from where I stood. It wasn't a hill, just a little more than a swelling, as though the earth had breathed and held it in.

When we said goodbye to the owner, he told us that the dog would be having puppies in a few weeks and if we liked to choose one, he'd happily make sure we'd get the pick of the litter.

Later, over dinner I suggested to Harry that Joseph might enjoy having his very own puppy.

'Maybe one day, Caitlin, but not while Bonza's still around.'

I never mentioned it again.

That same day, the mail brought news from Bridie. She and Kevin were all packed and should arrive at the Port of Melbourne around Easter time. Molly and Michael had become disenchanted by life at Oxford and had returned to the house at Langley. When I read that, I felt a lovely warm glow through my body. It was as if I understood that Patrick's home was intact. I smiled. I wept – just a little.

<h1 style="text-align:center">78</h1>

Caitlin

'Got news today,' Harry announced as he charged in the front door. 'In fact, I've got two pieces of news.'

'Tell me, tell me,' Caitlin shrieked.

'Nope. Gotta get cleaned up, get the ink off my hands, have a nice cup of tea, read today's paper.'

Caitlin grabbed his hands. 'They're perfectly clean.'

She made a grab for the papers in his hands. He dodged her attempt and charged along the passage to the sitting room, plonking himself on the sofa.

'Okay, come and sit for a minute. My boss Klon has been in touch with a Mr Curthoys, who's a leading member of the Australian Journalists Association. Klon has arranged a meeting for me to see this man in Melbourne. He'll be my mentor, send me minor assignments for a while, at least until I get better at the writing.'

'That's the perfect answer, Harry. You'll improve your qualifications without leaving home.'

'I'll need to go to Melbourne for assessment. You could come with me and we'll have a wee holiday. You'll like Melbourne. It rains a lot there – just like in England.'

I took off my hat and battered him with it. He laughed and grabbed me in a tight hold, where I stayed for a while.

The second piece of mail was from Frau Grottenthaler. A single page showed twelve lines of bold black script. In spite of faulty spelling, punctuation and grammar, we deduced that Nina had arrived in Australia (no date was stated); was getting settled in Shepparton, and getting confidence to write this letter had taken time; was happy with her life in Australia and was exploring possibilities of starting her own small business in preserving fruit as well as a cake/bread shop: she had chosen Shepparton because she learned there were a lot of fruit plantations there and a German society where she could have conversations in her own language.

Also it was near to Harry in Numurkah. It was her greatest wish to meet the man who'd kindly written to her after the war and who'd known her Karl. She wrote at the end, 'I am far, far beyond those beautiful days where I once watched roses and bluebells grow. I am mortally pierced with the dagger of Karl's death.'

It would make her very happy if Herr Kenihan would be kind enough to write to her at the address on the letter. The very next day, Saturday, Harry, Joseph and I set off for Shepparton. I wanted Harry to go on his own but he insisted.

'Best that we all go together, Caitlin. She can see us in our happiness and that will cheer her up.'

A short, plump elderly woman answered our knock on the door. She grinned and said, 'Hello. I'm Mrs Hutchinson. Can I be of any help to you? And what's your name, little boy?'

Joseph looked up at Harry, then at me, his eyes full of questions.

Harry introduced us. 'We're here to meet our German friend, Frau Grottenthaler.'

'Well then, you better come in. I'll call her. You sit in here.' She led the way to a sun-filled room where comfortable chairs dominated the space.

We heard clumping footsteps before Nina joined us. She grabbed Harry's hand and shook it as if she was pumping water from a well. Her eyes filled with tears.

When she looked down at Joseph, she bent almost to his height.

'*Mein Liebchen, danke.*'

Joseph grabbed a corner of my skirt and hid his face in the fabric.

She turned to me. 'He is…shy?' she asked.

'No, Nina, he's very tired.'

Nina was not pretty, but there was a freshness to her strong-boned face with its well-shaped mouth and cornflower-blue eyes, defined by eyebrows curved like a scythe on her brow.

Mrs Hutchison brought a tray laden with teacups, scones and little china dishes filled with jam and cream. 'Be back in a jiffy with the teapot,' she said. 'Make yourselves comfortable.

I asked Nina how she managed to get accommodation.

'My Villiam at the library in Deutschland help me very much. His English mother is known to the woman owner. You met her. I am renting one room here and she teaches me English, just like Villiam did. Herr Kenihan, tell me all about the night you met my Karl.'

It sounded like a command and, for Harry, it was unexpectedly early in the acquaintance. When he started to talk, his voice thickened and his face turned pale, as if he'd sped thousands of miles away to a disturbing memory. He wove a story about how Karl asked for his mother, and how Patrick felt a kinship with him when he saw the rosary. He said that Karl had died peacefully with a smile on his face.

'Well, Nina, I'm very pleased to have met you, but this little fella is getting restless and it's time to take him home. Next Saturday, I'll pick you up and bring you back to our home at Numurkah. You can tell us then about your plans for the future here in Australia. I'm very pleased to have met you.'

On the way home, I acknowledged the difference between what I'd heard before about Karl's death and the details he'd told Nina.

'Well, you know, m'dear, sometimes we have to embroider the truth in the name of kindness.'

I snuggled up close to him and gave thanks for having him beside me.

79

Harry

It was all arranged. A trip to Melbourne was essential. As it turned out, a visit to the university coincided with the arrival of Bridie and Kevin. Joseph jumped and clapped his hands and shouted 'Whoopee' when we told him we were going on a long train trip and that Bridie and Kevin were coming to live in Numurkah. We were booked into the railway hotel for two nights.

On the first morning, I set off for my appointment just as the skies dumped the contents of massive black bladders on the city streets, and on me. Fortunately, the package holding a selection of articles I'd written and my boss's recommendation were safely tucked in my inside jacket pocket.

A little old bearded man behind a desk at the entrance directed me to the appropriate office. By the time I'd tramped, meandered, strolled, stomped along a convoluted menagerie of corridors, my hair and most of my jacket were dry.

It wasn't an interview as much as a lecture on the expectations required of me and how privileged I should feel to be accepted. The offer of entry was compensation for my effort in the war. I thought it odd that he didn't open the package with samples of my writing – I shouldn't have bothered.

He grumped, 'You will receive a formal acceptance and your first term's work within the next week or so. Goodbye.' Then a loud 'hrumph' from the back of his throat.

Caitlin and Joseph had gone to the museum and when I met up

with them, Joseph and I competed for Caitlin's ear for the retelling of our separate stories about dinosaurs; thin drawers filled with butterflies; getting soaked in the rain; and dark carpeted passageways.

Early next morning, we caught a tram that took us almost to the dock where the ship bringing Bridie and Kevin waited, anchored and safe.

I whispered to Caitlin, 'Remember this place?'

'Yes, yes, I do. You wore a summer linen suit. Now you're wrapped up in a mac.'

'I remember still the first sight of your face. You still happy about your decision?

'Yes, Harry. I'm very contented, and getting more so each day. Thanks to you and to your mother.' She snuggled as close to me as much as the public space would allow.

We watched the initial unloading and organising of cabin trunks and suitcases but after a few minutes we changed our focus to passengers ranked along the rail shouting and waving at the crowd below. I heard a long loud, 'CAITLIN, HARRY!'

Joseph jumped up and down. The rain had stopped but Caitlin's cheeks were wet, her body shaking. Bridie waved a green and gold scarf as if she was claiming the entire continent for Ireland.

Later, on the train back to Numurkah, conversation was broken into fragments like stuff in a catch-all drawer.

There was nothing of England in Bridie. She and Kevin brought only the sounds and smells and songs of Ireland that were clearly stamped on their faces and in their voices.

80

Caitlin

On a night when the temperature had dropped to six degrees, Harry brought my winter jacket to me. 'Put this on, Caitlin, I'm going to show you something very special.'

This was one of many pillion rides on his beloved bike. We dodged potholes and veered away from tractor gouges until we passed the last tree in a long plantation of Norfolk pine trees. We drove to the top of a small rise.

Harry grinned from ear to ear as he helped me off the pillion seat. 'Now, Caitlin, close your eyes.'

I did.

He put one arm around my waist and his right hand on my arm. 'Just a few steps to a level spot.' He guided me slowly. 'Now tilt your head backwards.'

By this time, I was giggling nervously.

'Now, my love, open your eyes.'

I did. It was like being smack in the middle of the universe. The sky was ablaze with the light of millions of stars.

All I could say was, 'Ooooh.' I'd never seen a sky like it. 'Thank you, Harry.'

He still held on to me and we stood that way until my neck got a crick in it.

After a long loving kiss, Harry pointed up to a particular cluster of stars. 'See that long silver misty trail?'

'Yes.'

'That's the Milky Way and you won't see it any brighter than the way it is now. And can you spot four bright stars with a fifth one at the end?' He trailed his hand in a southerly direction.

'Yes, I can.'

'That's the Southern Cross.'

I was aware of being in some holy place, like a cathedral. No sound disturbed us, and the universe was completely ours.

'I will remember this always, Harry.'

'This will be our special place, Caitlin. When we feel the need for a beautiful space, this is where we'll find it.'

We stood silent for a long while, two bodies at one with the universe and each other.

Epilogue

Christmas 1924

Lettie's eyesight had faded and her sewing life ended. The ancient Singer sewing machine was relegated to a cupboard in the hallway and leftover swatches of fabrics bundled and bagged to wait for destiny's call. Caitlin, Harry and sometimes Joseph shared reading to her. Lettie favoured stories about successful migrants – especially those who came from her native Scotland.

Caitlin sympathised with her but Lettie, ever stalwart, chided her, 'Caitlin, as long as I have my garden and my sense of smell, I'll be happy. No need to worry about me.' Then she said, 'It's like the League of Nations in here. But we are all people under the skin.'

Harry's rendition of Paterson's 'Santa Claus in the Bush' briefly shifted Caitlin's thoughts to memories of Christmas 1918, but there was only joy when Harry announced that he and Caitlin were expecting their first child in June 1925.

Harry disliked the occasional trips to Melbourne – the smells and noise of the city bothered him – but he loved learning to get better at writing news stories about the people of Numurkah. He accepted an opportunity to buy a partnership in the *Numurkah Leader* and eventually became a valued member of the shire council.

Nina realised her dream of a little shop and selling the produce that she nurtured and preserved. She started a business in Shepparton that kept her busy and successful. Her jams and preserves were demanded throughout the eastern states of Australia. In time, she extended the premises and added bread and baked goods to the menu.

Bridie and Kevin never had any children of their own, but as Caitlin and Harry's brood grew, they became the family support team. Bridie was a second mother to Joseph, Kevin a favourite uncle.

A little boy learned to fly a kite, ride a billycart and sing "♪woo loo moo loo♪" to the tune of 'Ali Bali Bee'. He thrived in the wide-open spaces that surrounded him. He inherited his father's love of song and was happy to entertain anyone who'd listen to him sing.